It's Getting Dark

Also by Peter Stamm

It's
Getting
Dark

. . . s t o r i e s . . .

Peter Stamm

TRANSLATED FROM THE GERMAN
BY MICHAEL HOFMANN

OTHER PRESS
NEW YORK

We wish to express our appreciation to the Swiss Arts Council Pro Helvetia
for their assistance in the preparation of this translation.

Production editor: Yvonne E. Cárdenas
Text designer: Jennifer Daddio
This book was set in Goudy Old Style and Gotham

1 3 5 7 9 10 8 6 4 2

Library of Congress Cataloging-in-Publication Data
Names: Stamm, Peter, 1963- author. | Hofmann, Michael, 1957 August 25- translator.
Title: It's getting dark : stories / Peter Stamm ; translated from the German
by Michael Hofmann.
Other titles: Wenn es dunkel wird. English | It is getting dark
Description: New York : Other Press, [2021] | "Marcia from Vermont was originally
published in German as Marcia aus Vermont: Eine Weihnachtsgeschichte in 2019
by S. Fischer Verlag GmbH, Frankfurt am Main. The other stories were originally
published in German as Wenn es dunkel wird: Erzählungen in 2020 by
S. Fischer Verlag GmbH, Frankfurt am Main."
Identifiers: LCCN 2021023446 (print) | LCCN 2021023447 (ebook) |
ISBN 9781635420302 (hardcover) | ISBN 9781635420319 (ebook)
Subjects: LCSH: Stamm, Peter, 1963- —Translations into English. |
LCGFT: Short stories.
Classification: LCC PT2681.T3234 W4613 2021 (print) | LCC PT2681.T3234 (ebook) |
DDC 833/.92—dc23
LC record available at https://lccn.loc.gov/2021023446
LC ebook record available at https://lccn.loc.gov/2021023447

Contents

*

Marcia from Vermont

I t wasn't exactly a mad dash, but I have to admit it was a relief to get out of the valley at the end of two months. Early on in my time there, I had once or twice climbed one of the hills in the vicinity for a change of perspective, but there was nothing to see but other, higher hills and wooded mountainsides. Then, once the weather turned at the beginning of December and the snow came, there was no possibility of getting anywhere except by tramping along the plowed roads. Even on the foundation's grounds there was nowhere to walk except the footpaths connecting the individual buildings, which were kept clear by some mysterious agency.

I could have saved myself the expense of the rental car, I made no use of it at all during my time there, but then I hadn't known how else I was going to get from New York City to this place in the back of beyond. On the morning of my departure I was a long time looking in the big parking lot behind the main building before I saw it, buried under deep snow that took me the best part of an hour to clear away sufficiently that I could get into it and drive. When I went back to my room to pick up my bags, my hands were red and swollen from the cold. I went in the bathroom and held them under the cold tap. It felt like the pricks of a hundred needles.

I drove off, without seeing or speaking to anyone. Most of the others had left already and I hadn't had dealings with any of them much, nor with the staff, who did their work but otherwise seemed to keep themselves to themselves. The young woman who laid out the breakfast buffet every morning and who replied to my greeting with a nod and some incomprehensible mutter, I had never heard to speak at all. Only sometimes I saw her whispering to one of the cooks, with an expression on her face as though she had just seen or experienced something absolutely awful.

The car skidded on the icy driveway, but the actual road was happily in good condition. There was just one spot behind a bend where my lane was buried under

a heap of snow that must have slid off the steep side
of a hill overnight. I had to brake sharply and use the
opposite lane.

I had thought I would stop for breakfast at the
first coffee shop on my way, but the places I passed
all looked uninviting, and I was driving for an hour
before I saw somewhere that looked semi-civilized. But
even that turned out to have just the usual shrink-
wrapped bagels and gluey muffins with watery coffee.
The person at the till asked me where I was from and
if I was here on vacation, but I didn't feel like talking,
or had forgotten how, during the past weeks of silence.
And that, even though I'd been looking forward to my
stay at the foundation and had been longing for exactly
what I found there, tranquillity, a place outside of time,
and nothing to keep me from my work.

There was nothing on the radio except a couple
of geezers yacking about car repairs, to their vast
amusement. I punched through the stations till I
found one that was playing jazz, interrupted by the odd
weather update and ads for water beds and agricultural
machinery. I thought of Marcia, and how we'd met one
Christmas many years ago. I was very young at the
time and had gone to New York full of ambition. But
before a single year was up, I was out of money, and I
had achieved nothing and nothing seemed any closer

to being realized, and I had to write to my parents for money for the flight home. They had hoped I would be back for the holidays, but probably from sheer cussedness I had booked my flight for early January. I spent Christmas with a Brazilian couple I knew in Queens, and their kids; I had no idea I would never see them again. I have no memory of the occasion, but it must have been lunchtime, because when I left my friends' place, it still wasn't dark.

I was slightly the worse for wear, and thought I'd walk it off. I stopped at a corner to get my bearings. I had just lit a cigarette when a woman accosted me and asked if I had one to spare. When I lit it for her, she sweetly cupped her hands around mine. She looked at me and smiled. It was her birthday, she said, and if I had twenty dollars, we could buy a few things and party.

"Sorry," I said, "that's more than I've got."

She said that didn't matter, and I should wait for her there. She'd go to the shop, and would be back in a second.

"Fancy having your birthday on Christmas day."

"I guess," she said, as though it hadn't occurred to her. "There is that."

She walked off down the street, and I knew it wasn't her birthday and that she wouldn't come back. "Wait," I called out, and quickly bounded up to her.

She made her purchases like someone who was hungry, high-calorie foods, cheap brands, big packets, no fruit or veg. To begin with she kept count of the total, told me what it was, and looked at me. "That's okay," I said finally, "I've still got one or two travelers' checks." I put a bottle of cheap whiskey in the trolley. "Why not?"

Her place was in a decrepit-looking house down a dark side street. We walked up four flights of stairs. There was a weird smell I couldn't place, but even weirder was the total silence on all sides. You couldn't even hear the street anymore, just the creaking of the treads which was so loud you thought they might collapse at any moment. In the apartment it was cold and dark. We kept our coats on as we ate in her kitchen, white bread with peanut butter and sliced turkey. Finally, when she had had enough, she got up, took off her coat, and looked at me with a mixture of sadness and challenge. "Are you a saint?" she said. "That would frighten me even more."

"I've had too much to drink," I said.

She grinned. "I would have too, if I could afford it."

"But it's your birthday."

"Right," she said, "I almost forgot."

———

I don't remember the color of Marcia's hair or eyes, or if she was short or tall, curvaceous or slim. Nevertheless, I think I would recognize her if I ran into her on the street. There was a confidence and directness about her that impressed and attracted me.

We were lying in her bed. The blanket was thin, and I pressed against her, less to be close to her as simply not to be cold. "I don't make a habit of this, you know," she said, and suddenly started laughing. "You don't care, do you? But I really don't. Christmas is the saddest day in the calendar, and I've got no money and I didn't want to go to bed hungry."

The whiskey had loosened her tongue and made her sentimental. She talked about her family in Vermont, whom she hadn't seen for years, and her brother, her little handicapped brother, as she said.

"You don't mean that, do you?" I said. "That sounds like one of those awful Christmas sob stories. You sleep with me to get money to pay his prescription drugs. And at the end, we all of us sit together around a scrawny Christmas tree and sing carols, you and I, your parents, and your little handicapped brother."

"My little brother's been dead for a long time," she said, "and my father's stinking rich, and I have no intention of introducing you to him."

For a while neither of us spoke. "Is your name really Marcia?" I asked. "I thought it was just people on TV had names like that."

"Why wouldn't it be?" she said. Again, no one spoke, then Marcia asked me what my most unusual Christmas was. I sensed she had had a fair few herself and was only asking me to get a chance to tell me about them. "Marcia from Vermont," I said. "You're probably my strangest Christmas present."

I lit cigarettes for us both. Marcia reached across me to fill our glasses. Her breasts brushed against my arm. "I know I've had worse whiskey," she said. I pulled her down on top of me. "What's that?" she asked. "O Christmas tree, O Christmas tree..."

I must have been asleep. It was pitch dark, and I had no idea what the time was. Marcia was still awake, in the dark I heard her voice very close to my ear, as though she hadn't stopped talking. "Tell me, what was the strangest Christmas you've ever had?" she repeated, as though it was an important question, and everything depended on my answer.

"Maybe I haven't had it yet," I said. "This is the first Christmas I've spent away from home."

"Maybe it will seem unusual to you one day," she said.

"And what about you?" I asked, reaching for her. In spite of the chill room, her body felt feverishly hot. "Come closer," I said, pulling her toward me. "Aren't you tired?"

"I never sleep," she said. Her laugh sounded half eerie, half amused.

"And are your parents really rich?" I asked.

"Loaded," she said, laughing.

I got up and stumbled through the darkness to the toilet in a passage which was even colder than the bedroom. When I returned, Marcia had lit a candle end on a saucer by the side of the bed. She lay on her back and flung open the bedding. "Come on," she said, "this woman needs a lot of loving." I didn't have the impression Marcia needed a lot of loving at all. There was a silent tussle between us, she twisted in my arms, gripped me, but I kept feeling part of her was still uninvolved, or rather, as though she was watching us while we were making love. She sat on top of me, pressed me down on the bed, and looked at me with a strange smile. I was surprised by her strength. Marcia laughed. "Where I'm from, women have to be strong."

The candle seemed to flare up briefly, then with a soft hiss it went out, and we lay in complete darkness again. In the last of its light, Marcia's face seemed to have caught a glow, and briefly her features looked altogether soft, as though she was thinking of something, or remembering some moment of happiness. She laid her head on my chest and said, "We used to have the most amazing Christmases." Marcia's father was the publisher of a newspaper, but the family had been moneyed for several generations, I don't remember where the money came from, or if Marcia even told me. She had grown up in Burlington, but the family had spent holidays and vacations in a village in the Green Mountains, in an old grain mill on a stream. She had had a brother who was a couple of years younger than she was, and he did have a slight disability. When he was five or six, he died, and it was her fault. She was supposed to look after him, but had read a book or fallen asleep instead, I don't remember. Had he drowned in the stream, or fallen somewhere? Or am I just imagining all that, and in fact he died of his condition? All I can really remember is the way Marcia always laughed when she talked about sad things. She told me most of her life story that night. I don't remember if I told her mine as well, my ambitions, my various attempts, my reverses. "Lots of people fancy themselves as artists," I said, "it doesn't mean anything."

"My boyfriend is a writer," said Marcia.

"You've got a boyfriend?" I asked in consternation.

"Occasionally."

As I say, this was all a long time ago, thirty years at least. I had forgotten a lot of it, and what I remembered probably didn't have much to do with what actually happened.

For over two hours I'd been driving through sparsely inhabited country on small back roads, mostly woods and farmland, occasional small towns that didn't seem to have much more going on in them than places back home. At the time I was living in New York, I hardly ever left the city, and on subsequent visits to the States, I'd only ever been in cities. I barely knew rural America, and I was amazed by how backward and impoverished it seemed to be. I was glad when somewhere near the state boundary I finally hit the interstate. I would make more rapid progress and wouldn't have to concentrate so hard.

The following days really were among the strangest in my life, it was as though all the rules and conventions were briefly invalidated, and for a short time everything was possible. When I woke up the next morning, I was lying alone in bed. From the kitchen I could hear voices, Marcia's and a man's. I got up and pulled on my clothes. I was just trying to sneak out of the apartment when a man, wearing a suit and a little older than me apparently, stepped into the corridor.

"You must be Peter," he said. "Do you want some coffee? I brought some for you." I followed him into the kitchen, where Marcia was fiddling with a coffee maker. There was a packet of Dean & DeLuca coffee on the kitchen table.

"Meet David," Marcia said, "my writer friend I was telling you about." David, laughing, apologized for not having introduced himself. But he was part of the furniture, and accordingly he sometimes forgot himself. There was something starchy about the way he spoke, and I instinctively took against him; even so, I felt drawn to him. It's often that way with me and people who are more self-assured than I am and seem to know what they're about.

Later on that day, as I remember, we visited David's place. He had a very beautiful wife whose name I've forgotten, I think she was French, and it was Michelle or Mireille. When we arrived, the Polish home helper was just leaving to take the two kids sledding in Central Park. I remember that neither kids nor helper put in another appearance, nor in the days to come when I was there to see David and Michelle/Mireille.

The apartment was stylishly furnished with very large windows that in my memory seem like the ones in *Rear Window*, but I could be mistaken about that, in fact I'm pretty sure I am. I have no recollection of a Christmas tree, but I do remember a smoked glass coffee table that had a few picture books lying out on it. After I'd finished browsing through one and put it back, David adjusted its position, as though everything here had to be just so. I remember David showing me how to make a proper martini, and that we didn't stop after just one.

The conversation was about love and relationships. Marcia, David, and Michelle/Mireille seemed to be in a kind of *ménage à trois* whose rules and details I never quite understood, but that seemed more attractive to me the more I'd had to drink. Above all, what's left of that afternoon is a powerful sense of freedom, such as I have rarely felt before or since. During those hours everything seemed to me possible and permissible, everything was correct and good. In the days ahead, we spent a lot of time together in varying configurations. Once I went out to Coney Island with Marcia and Michelle/Mireille and because it was so cold, we took a hotel room and holed up there all afternoon. When we handed in the key, the porter passed some remark, but we just laughed, we couldn't care less what he thought of us. One evening I spent alone with David in his apartment, while Marcia and Michelle/Mireille were away somewhere, and only returned very late and in high old spirits. One time, when I was briefly home and rang Marcia, she said she had a date with David and his wife, and when I asked if I could come too, she fobbed me off. I started to make a little jealousy scene, but she was adamant. And then the next day Michelle/Mireille visited my studio. She had been out shopping, and said she just wanted to warm up a bit, but she ended up staying fully two hours. The wretchedness of my premises seemed to stimulate her, she spent the entire time laughing. "Better not tell David I was here," she said, getting dressed. For New Year's Eve we were together, all four of us, and then our relationship ended as abruptly as it had begun. We spent the night celebrating at David and Michelle/Mireille's; to my memory, the apartment is full of people, but maybe I'm mistaken, and it was just the four of us. We were drinking and dancing, playing strange games that suddenly turned serious, then one of the women would burst out laughing, and everything broke up. As it got light, I went off, without mentioning the fact that I was about to go home or telling the others my address or phone number in Switzerland. I never saw any of them again. My life resumed its sway.

At the time I met Marcia, my life was in the doldrums. Then, once I was back in Switzerland, things got straightened out, and in the years ahead all my hopes came to fruition, as the saying goes. But that's another story. I didn't often think about my year in New York, only sometimes when I was visiting my parents at Christmas—those peculiar holidays that were really one long celebration, a celebration of freedom and youth and endless possibilities. Years passed before I was next in New York, and by then the city had changed for me. This time, I visited museums and galleries, rode around in taxis, and ate in restaurants without anxiously looking at the prices first. I had everything money could buy, but not the feeling of freedom I had had before.

My German gallerist had given me the number of a colleague of his in New York. We met up for coffee and talked about the art scenes in our respective countries, and artists we knew and liked, or knew and disdained, and finally about a possible exhibition for me, but everything remained rather up in the air. "There are loads of possibilities," the gallerist said. Then he told me about an artists' colony in Vermont. He was on the application committee. "Why don't you apply," he said. "Spend a couple of months in Vermont. Work or relax, suit yourself, no one will mind. The food is

good, and the landscape is gorgeous." The name of
the foundation sounded vaguely familiar, but only
when the gallerist told me the history of the place did
I realize it was Marcia's family who had founded the
colony, that this was the place with the old mill where
she had spent part of her childhood. "The family lost
a child," said the gallerist. "After that tragedy, they
deeded the property to a foundation for the arts. Over
time they've bought up several more houses in the
village. The woman died a few years ago, but the man
and his daughter still live there. He must be well over
eighty."

Nothing ever came of the New York show, but I was
so busy I hardly cared. Only when I found myself
at a loose end at the completion of a major project,
the artists' colony sprang to mind. I applied for one
of the scholarships, and shortly afterward received
notification that I had been accepted. Ideally, I would
have set off for Vermont immediately, but the vacancies
they had were in November and December, and that
was fine by me. When the time came, I flew to New
York, rented a car, and set off.

Before my arrival there, I hadn't received much
in the way of information from the colony, just a map

of the location, and a bizarrely detailed set of house rules full of ridiculous formulations that threw up more questions than answers. I had driven all day and arrived in the late afternoon as it was getting dark. I parked behind the mill, which seemed more like a factory to me, a vast wooden complex that had evidently been added to over the years, and followed a sign marked RECEPTION. The foundation office was in a little wooden cabin with large windows that had probably once housed a store. The door was open, but there was no one around. On the counter lay an envelope with my name on it.

Next to the office was a small gallery, also unlocked, and bathed in bright light. On the floor lay curious installations made from tree branches and bones and skins. On the rear wall was a framed piece of paper bearing the artist's name and a brief first-person biography. He was a descendant of the Cowasuck Indians, who had lived here in former times, wrote this man named Jeremy Muhn. He went through the phases of his life, which were no more unusual than any other artist's biography. Right at the end came sentences that referred to his ethnicity again: "There are many of us among you in all areas of life. If we didn't tell you about ourselves, you wouldn't know the first thing about us."

I opened the envelope and found a key and a map
of the colony. Around the old mill, which contained
various common spaces, a library, and a refectory
(along with a laundry room and a bicycle garage in
the basement), there were at least half a dozen houses
containing studios, workshops, office rooms, and a
deconsecrated church that was used for events. One of
the houses at the edge of the terrain was marked with a
red cross, and next to it I read: YOUR PLACE.

My studio was in a white-painted wooden building
of the sort I'd seen in countless American films. It
had a screen door and a porch with a rocking chair.
It looked a little run-down and could have done with
a fresh coat of paint. Inside were four studios, two
on the ground floor, two more upstairs. My key ring
bore the number of one of the upstairs studios, which
turned out to be a big room with a vast double bed, a
sitting area, and an old-fashioned writing desk. There
was an ancient TV set perched on an old chest of
drawers, and in a corner of the room a cooking area
with small fridge, coffee machine, and microwave.
There were even a few provisions, instant coffee,
black tea, oatmeal, and a can of noodle soup. Next to
the fridge, a door opened onto the bathroom, which

contained a small tub and a loose towel rack. The window had been cracked open and freezing air was coming in.

There were fresh towels on the bed and an extra wool blanket, and on the desk there were some mimeographed sheets with further information, mealtimes, emergencies and so forth, a list of important phone numbers, and Internet instructions. You could pick up a modem in the office, it said, along with a username and password.

The walls were decorated with framed black-and-white photographs that presumably showed life in an earlier incarnation of the colony, happy people celebrating, pictures at concerts and other events, hikes and swimming trips to the creek. One photograph showed about a score of people around a huge Christmas tree; what was strange here was that they were all in costume and masks, as though they were coming from a ball, or were on their way to one. There was an old, white-haired man in many of the photographs, I assumed he was Marcia's father, the man who had started the foundation. In one of the older photographs I saw him next to a young woman, with his arm draped over her shoulder. I wondered if that might be Marcia, but I couldn't for the life of me remember what she looked like.

I put my clothes away in the big wardrobe in the bedroom and laid out my drawing things on the desk. Mechanically, I rummaged through the drawers, which except for a bit of dust were empty: a cent, a hairpin, a rusty lock without a key. Then, lying in the top one, I found a manuscript that looked as though it had been put there for me.

The cover sheet had just the title on it, "A Christmas Story," in quotation marks. There was no author's name either at the beginning or at the end, but the further I read in the story, the more certain I was that the author was David, the writer boyfriend to whom Marcia had introduced me so many years ago. I seemed to recognize his pretentiousness, his irony and his cool.

It was all about the time when I had met first Marcia and then David and his wife. The author had altered all our names, so that Marcia was Mary, he called me Joseph, and he and his wife were Dean and Lucy. Joseph, or sometimes merely "the Swiss guy," was the villain, who had broken into a blissful erotic triangle and destroyed it. Triangles were stable, it said somewhere in the story, rectangles were not. David must have written this thing years after the event, that was the only way I could explain the

difference between his recollection and mine, and
presumably the facts such as they were. There was
none of the lightness and sense of freedom that I
had experienced. He described me as aggressive and
intrusive, claimed I had come on to both Marcia and
Michelle/Mireille, or in the story, Mary and Lucy. At
the same time, he talked about things he could only
have known about because he had heard about them
from the two women, intimate details I wouldn't even
have told my best friend. David's wife didn't cut a
particularly good figure in the story either. I had sensed
the tension between them right away. In the story,
David wrote about her with a crudeness that took
my breath away. Lucy was a spoiled Frenchwoman,
a ballerina who dreamed of great success but was far
too indolent to do anything about it. Nor did she look
after the children either, instead she spent her days
hanging around in the city, spending Dean's money
and meeting other men. Marcia or Mary, meanwhile,
was the dream of an American woman, practical and
kind, intelligent and full of drive. If what the story
said was true, then Marcia and David had first met as
children in a summer camp in Vermont. They came
from affluent families presumably, and for both of
them it was a sort of harmless puppy love, but David
at any rate seemed convinced they were destined for

one another. The prehistory of Mary, Dean, and Lucy
was left fragmentary, so it never became clear why
Dean and Mary never became a couple, or why they
had entered into that *menage à trois* with Lucy that so
fascinated me. The story had something dishonest and
overheated about it, it was like the belated confession
of a remorseful sinner. What was curious was the way
David wrote about Dean, his alter ego. He seemed
utterly different from my sense of him at the time, a
sensitive young man, highly gifted but ill equipped for
life, beset and manipulated from all sides.

There were about twenty pages of this story. The
handwriting became increasingly wild, and as I went
on, it felt less and less like a story and more and more
like a screed, an accusation. On the last few pages,
presumably out of negligence, David had lapsed into
using our actual names, so I finally saw that his wife
was called Michelle and not Mireille, only what he was
writing remained utterly false to me. Most of all I was
astonished by the bitterness with which he wrote about
it all, as though the events hadn't happened in some
long-ago time, but their effects were still with us. The
emotions were so fresh, as though the narrator felt
everything as powerfully as he might have done then,
his love for Marcia, his contempt for Michelle, his
hatred for me. It wasn't till I got to the last page that

I understood why that was so. After my departure the relationship of the other three rapidly disintegrated; it was no longer the stable triangle it had been earlier. Dean and Lucy got divorced, while he and Mary for some reason didn't get together either and ended up drifting apart. In its final lines the story recovered some of its initial chill. The last sentence was "A child was born."

The story caused me to miss supper. By the time I walked into the dining hall, there was no one there, only a girl in a white apron who was clearing away the buffet and replied to my greeting with a shy nod. I barely had time to get myself a bowl of soup and a couple of pieces of bread out of a big wooden crate.

In the time since my arrival I hadn't seen anyone but this girl, and now she was gone too. As she left, she turned down the light in the hall, and so I ate my sparse meal alone and in near-darkness. Somewhere in the building someone was playing the piano, and I could hear the rushing of the creek outside that must once have been used to drive the mill; otherwise it was silent.

On the bulletin board next to the entrance I saw that a Chinese composer was going to give a talk in the church tonight about her work and play a few samples of it. But I didn't really feel like company, maybe I was afraid I might run into Marcia or David. I was thinking about the end of the story as well, "A child was born." I wondered which of the women had become pregnant, and by whom. Would Marcia not have told me if the child was mine? Then again, how could she even know? Not to mention finding me. In those days hardly anyone used the Internet and to find me in Switzerland with nothing to go on but my name would have taken unusual initiative and determination. For the first time, I counted back how long ago it was that I had known Marcia. It was thirty-two years.

Outside Albany I stopped at a service station and filled up the car and ate a sandwich in the café. The thing was so vast, I could barely manage half of it. I looked at the other diners, wondered where they came from, where they were going to, what the purpose of their journey was, what their story was. A lot of them were presumably going home to their families, to have Christmas together. I didn't envy them. I would rather be alone than in some indifferent company, and I had no living close family anymore, at least that had been my belief until recently. On my way up here, I had stopped and eaten somewhere nearby, but then I had still been full of anticipation and drive, as was often the way at the beginning of trips. The weeks ahead of me were like a promise, a promise that wasn't kept.

I had resolved in my two months here to thoroughly explore the area, and gain some fresh ideas, but the days and weeks had slipped past without me doing or achieving much of anything. I read, I sketched, I watched TV. There were always a lot of people around at mealtimes, employees of the foundation and visiting artists. For the most part they were much younger than me, and since they had arrived before me, they had formed into groups, and I had no desire to join one. I sat now at one table, now at another, but never managed more than a little polite chitchat. Perhaps the young artists were nervous because they had heard of me, but I don't really think any of them knew about me. The art world is full of little movements and groupings and for ambitious young artists it's almost obligatory to fail to acknowledge the work of their elders, and to show no interest in it. There were a few musicians in the colony, but they were almost more reclusive, and always disappeared after mealtimes to go and practice together or whatever they did. The most

sociable were the writers, who often trooped off to
the pub after supper. On one occasion, I agreed to go
along with them, but they didn't talk about anything
but money, money and books I hadn't read, so after a
couple of beers I made my excuses and pushed off back
to my studio. There was no further trace of David.
Once, I tried asking who had been in the studio
before me, only to be told it was some Romanian poet.
I didn't dare ask who else had access to the rooms,
the empty studios were kept unlocked as a matter of
course. Sometimes I thought the whole business with
the Christmas story was just a silly joke, up to and
including the child that had apparently been born. I
couldn't believe, I refused to believe that I had a child
somewhere that was grown up and had nothing in
common with me except some strands of DNA. Then
I remembered Marcia's handicapped little brother and
the two of them became a kind of vague creature,
neither girl nor boy, the idea of a child. I pictured
Marcia walking hand in hand with him, and it wasn't
quite clear who was protecting whom, which of them
needed the other more.

I never saw the man who had started the foundation,
and when others talked about him, it was always in a

veiled way. No one seemed to know much about him, they hadn't even met him. The people who worked for the foundation didn't mention him out of principle. He kept an apartment at the back of the mill building, I managed to ascertain, with a separate entrance and a private garden behind a high hedge. At first, I was told he was away in New York, fundraising, but even when there was an old Land Rover parked outside, and there were lights on in his apartment, I never once bumped into him anywhere.

The person I saw the most of was a woman called Tracy, who worked in reception, and who seemed to be responsible for pretty much everything that went on in the place. She gave me the modem for the Internet and told me where to do my laundry, she helped me fill out some financial forms and she gave me my mail. Once when my toilet was blocked, she got hold of a plumber and when it started to snow, she warned me about black ice and snow off the roofs. Sometimes I went around to reception just for a bit of a chat with her, so that I didn't completely disappear in my solitude. Then we would get to talking about American politics or the weather, or she would tell me about local events, the beginning of the hunting season or the construction of a new bridge somewhere, lots of trifling things, till eventually she would say, Okay, and get back to work.

When I asked her about the benefactor, Tracy gave evasive replies, but I could feel that she had a great regard for him and seemed devoted to him. Once I asked her straight out about Marcia.

"Do you remember her then?" she asked, and suddenly her voice sounded somehow cold.

"From another life," I said.

"I haven't seen her in ages," said Tracy.

"Does she live here still?" I asked.

Just then the mailman walked in, and Tracy got drawn into a conversation about some parcel for an artist who had left already. I waved to the pair of them and walked off.

The foundation was at the edge of a village that didn't consist of much more than a main road with a bar and a few shops, and a few unpaved roads that went up the hills to either side, flanked with wooden houses. At the far end of the village was a little market where I bought most of my meals, precooked things I warmed up in the microwave and ate in my room.

The village people seemed to be reserved about the foundation. On the one hand the little businesses did make their living from us guests, and from the kitchen which made a point of using exclusively locally sourced products, but whenever I was in one of the shops, I felt the locals' suspicion of artists, some of whom, to make matters worse, were from abroad. The friendliest of them was Hilda, the old bookseller, who was not from here herself, and had somehow got stuck here on account of some romantic episode, if I remember correctly. It was a tiny shop, but she had a surprisingly good selection, with a shelf of secondhand books and even one of poetry books. I went around there once. She was on the phone, and I browsed through the old selection. I pulled out a thin yellow volume whose title made me curious: *A Map of Verona*. It was a book of poems that had come out just after the end of the war, the poet was an English fellow I'd never heard of. I flicked through it, started reading here and there, and had the weird feeling that the poems were all about me and Marcia, our first encounter, and now my time here. "The Return" was the title of one of them, and it was about a Christmas morning:

> *We have been off on a long voyage, have we not?*
> *Have done and seen much in that time, but have got*
> *Little that you will prize.*

Another one was called "Outside and In" and began with the words:

Suddenly I knew that you were outside the house,
The trees were silent you were prowling among.
A twig snapped, the birds in the garden fell silent.
Why have you come? Have you come in peace?
Or have you come to blackmail me,
Or just to gain knowledge?

"What have you got there?" asked Hilda when I
went to pay, and she turned it in her hands this way
and that, as though she'd never seen it before. "Shall
we say ten dollars?"

We talked for a while, then, frustrated by Tracy's
evasive replies, I tried asking Hilda about the daughter
of the foundation's president. But she couldn't or
wouldn't say much either. Only that Marcia had
achieved a degree of celebrity a few years ago as a
photographer. "There was a minor scandal," she said.
"She published a book of photographs that in certain
quarters was found to be too intimate. The most fuss
was about some pictures of her daughter."

On some of the photographs, the little girl had
been completely naked, Hilda told me, though
they were harmless and actually rather lovely and
aesthetically pleasing pictures. But the book had
precipitated a huge debate about abuse and pedophilia.

Which admittedly hadn't harmed sales. But after that not much had been heard from Marcia.

I asked Hilda if she stocked it. She shook her head. "But I can look on the Internet for you," she said. "I'm sure I'll find a copy somewhere."

As I left the shop, the sun was just peeping out behind the clouds. I walked through the village, passed the supermarket, and headed on west along the creek. I tried to remember Marcia. I remembered that she had taken pictures even then. The time the three of us were in Coney Island, she kept following us with a little box camera. Michelle had posed for her, though Marcia kept telling us she wanted us to behave perfectly naturally, and to just pretend she wasn't there. I can picture her standing there, feet apart, the camera masking her face. I asked: Did she want me to smile? She shook her head. "No," she said. "Just like that. That's perfect."

Oddly enough, I felt as though I'd seen the pictures at the time, even though Marcia was using film and certainly hadn't had the shots developed and printed during the brief time we knew each other. Perhaps it was just my memory, black-and-white shots, me sitting on a rock, smoking, and Michelle leaning against me in the howling gale, or the pair of us lying naked on the bed in the tacky hotel room we had ended up taking out of some whim, Michelle now looking serious and

me with an expression on my face that I don't even like
to think about.

The valley widened out, and now there was grazing
land as well as forest. I wondered where I would get to
if I kept on going, but just then it started to rain, and I
turned back.

I spent the afternoon looking up Marcia. The
Internet connection was incredibly slow, and most
of the time I was just sitting in front of the computer
waiting for a page to come up, only to see right away
that I'd ended up down another rabbit hole. There was
very little there anyway, the time of Marcia's success
was long ago now, before everything was preserved a
thousand-fold online. Strangely, my sense of her got
vaguer and washier the more I found out about her.
The life I read about was not the life of the woman I
had known and who only existed in memory. It was as
though every deed, every experience, every incident
only subtracted from it, as though we had been much
more ourselves back then, foolish and immature as
we were. I had been much too ready to believe the
commonplace that a biography gets richer the longer it
carries on. If anything, the opposite was the case. Every
decision taken destroyed a hundred other possibilities
and in the end we all got to the same place, and
dissolved into nothing.

As I switched off the computer, I noticed how dark it had gotten in the room and how quiet it had become. When I got up and walked over to the window, I saw that the rain had turned into snow, and the grass and trees were already white. It was suppertime. My fridge was empty, but I didn't feel like eating with the others. At least I still had a bottle of whiskey. I drank much too quickly, and by nine I was so tired and drunk I lay down on my bed and was quickly asleep.

When I woke up the following morning, it was still snowing, and it went on all week. My walks were confined to the supermarket at the end of the village and back. Sometimes I went to the pub in the daytime, just to get out of the studio and have a bit of company.

This was early December, but the bulletin board in the dayroom already announced the big Christmas party. The president of the foundation was playing host. "All welcome," it said on the sheet, "regardless of whether you've been good or bad."

Hilda had indeed managed to get hold of a copy of Marcia's book of photographs for me, secondhand, bearing an undated dedication, "To Peter," and below it, Marcia's name.

"Funny," said Hilda, "your name. But of course you share it with a few others."

I asked her where she had got hold of it. It was from some online source of used books, she said. No mention had been made of the dedication. She had just wanted a copy in good condition and fairly inexpensive. "These kind of pictures are popular with a certain class of people," she said. "It wasn't easy to find the book."

I quickly bagged it and hurried back to my studio. I locked the door behind me, as though I was afraid I was doing something unlawful.

The book was called *Extended Family*, and it had come out fourteen years after Marcia and I had met. On the jacket there was a photo of Michelle and David and two children, presumably taken in Central Park. The thing that distinguished it from a conventional family portrait was that everyone was looking in a different direction, as though they lived in separate worlds, and it was pure chance that they had happened to appear at one and the same time in front of the photographer's lens.

Most of the pictures in the first half of the book were interiors, and they showed couples doing perfectly mundane things, washing the dishes or in the bath or watching TV, though a lot of them were naked or partially naked, and a few of the couples were lesbian or gay. The pictures were in black and white and contrived to look at one and the same time casual and composed. I wondered if they had indeed been posed and remembered how Marcia had once photographed me and Michelle, spending minutes with the camera in front of her face waiting to click the shutter at the right moment, like a hunter waiting for his quarry to show its vulnerable point. Then I saw the photo of Michelle and me, and I felt the recollection of that day flooding over me, not so much what had happened on it so much as the mood, which hadn't by any means been as untroubled as I'd thought. Marcia was lying in bed in her underwear reading a magazine, I was standing naked in the window which I'd opened a crack, smoking a cigarette. You couldn't see my face, but my posture was expressive of tension, irritation, or impatience. But the photos that had made the book so scandalous were in the second half, which was called "A Child Is Born." They were pictures of Marcia's daughter, again in perfectly ordinary situations, playing, showing off some injury, asleep. The earliest pictures had been taken immediately after her birth, and showed a tiny, yelling creature that seemed more like a wild animal than a human being. There followed pictures of the girl as a baby, as a toddler, taking her

first steps, in kindergarten. She has cut her knee and
is staring incredulously at the blood running down her
leg. While the pictures in the first part were taken in
city apartments, the setting now was a clapboard house
presumably out in the country somewhere. There was an
overgrown garden, woods, a riverbank. By the end of the
series, the girl was almost a teenager, her expression had
changed, now she looked sensitive, sometimes irked, as
though to say to the photographer, please stop, leave me
in peace. In some of the pictures the girl was naked, and
that was maybe what caused the scandal, the fact that it
was a perfectly ordinary, unprotected nakedness, not an
erotic pose that ended up showing the onlooker much
less. When I had looked up Marcia on the Internet the
previous day, I had come upon an incensed newspaper
article accusing her of child abuse. The illustration
for the article was a photograph of a girl of five or six
standing in an inflatable pool in the garden, launching a
little plastic boat into the water. The newspaper editors
had blacked out her eyes, nipples, and sex, which made
the perfectly innocent picture something sinful, turning
it into a piece of evidence in a trial, and making a victim
of the girl. I had found an interview with Marcia where
she spoke up for herself, saying when she took pictures of
the girl, they were not mother and daughter, but artist
and model.

"I don't have childhood memories, the way other people do," Marcia said in the interview. "Sometimes I think my only recollections are ones I've built up around childhood pictures of me. I get the impression I've constructed a past for myself. I am suspicious of my memories; I think they might be invented."

I looked closely at the girl in the photographs, looking for resemblances to me, or to David or Marcia, even though I could hardly remember what she looked like. I found nothing, she could have been any random girl. It didn't really matter either, because this girl no longer existed anyway, by now she was a woman in middle age with her own history and her own memories of a life that had gone ahead without me. What would have united us, if we'd ever met? The role Marcia played in our respective lives? But even Marcia existed in different versions for both of us, she was a chance lover for me, a mother for her. At the end of the interview, Marcia had declared she would go on taking pictures, but she wouldn't publish them anymore. "My art is my art," she said. "I'd rather it didn't exist than that it should be misunderstood."

At the end of the book was a brief, bland text by David. Since I now knew his surname, I was able to search the Internet for him as well. Again, there wasn't much, and what I found was contradictory. The

Wikipedia entry on him was presumably his own work, and it was much too exhaustive, given the tiny handful of things he had had published, listing every local grant and prize and every obscure publication. There was nothing about his private life. On the site of a local Burlington paper I found an obituary for someone bearing the same name that had appeared a few years back. The ages tallied, but I couldn't be sure it was about the same man. The deceased had taught at some college, there was nothing about his having been a writer.

In spite of the heavy snow, I was making good progress. As I neared my final destination, the area became more and more built up, and there was heavy traffic on the roads. Finally, the George Washington Bridge loomed up in front of me. Back when I had lived in the city, I had once lived for a time in an apartment right next to the bridge, along with a Colombian woman and a couple of Chinese ophthalmologists. But the unabating noise of traffic had driven me mad, and in the search for a quieter place, I had moved out to Queens.

Once I had crossed the bridge into Manhattan, I felt I was in another world, and my time at the foundation and everything I had done in the past couple of months seemed like a dream. Or maybe I was just trying to repress it all, to forget it, and carry on living, as though nothing had happened, and everything was just the way it had been before. For the first time in a long time I felt in the mood to work, my gallerist had got in touch shortly before the holidays, and there was talk of a possible show in the summer. I had talked to him about a couple of ideas I had, and he was quite enthusiastic. I wasn't in the mood for more memories, all this old stuff, I wanted to forge ahead and not reminisce about a life I wasn't in a position to change anyway. But as I drove through Queens, and streets with little wooden houses covered in snow that were not dissimilar to what I'd seen in Vermont, I was forced to think about the weeks just passed.

It had snowed for days. By the time it finally stopped, I was stir-crazy. I walked through the village, and because the sun was shining, I walked on down the plowed street. Where it curved to meet the creek— even though I was in town shoes—I tramped through deep snow down to the bank. A layer of ice had formed, though in some places you could see the water bubbling beneath.

I can see the creek in front of me, I put out a foot to test the ice, it cracks and breaks, and even though I pull back my foot immediately, I feel the instant chill of the water flooding my shoe. Perhaps it's a memory from childhood, the white air bubbles against the thin layer of ice, the dark flowing water, but the damp is real enough, the chill in my feet as I walk on through the snow not caring where I'm going, dazzled by the light of the sun reflected on the snow. My head hurts from so much light, and I feel dizzy, but there's nothing I could have grabbed onto, only the deep, soft snow. I stagger and fall to the side, laughing at my mishap, and at the same time stunned with light and cold. There is a gunshot in the distance, and then four more in quick succession, like the beat of an unheard music.

When I got back to the foundation it was almost dark. I was euphoric, but so cold that even in my overheated studio I was still gibbering, as though the cold had got into my bones. I ran a hot bath, poured myself a big glass of whiskey, and went to bed.

When I awoke, the light in the room was still on, and the whiskey glass was on the bedside table, untouched. My head ached, and I had a burning sensation in my forehead. I staggered to the bathroom, took an aspirin, and went back to bed.

I didn't feel any better the next morning. In addition to my headache, I had joint pains, and even though I felt cold, the bed was soaked in sweat. About

noon, I forced myself to get up and make some tea.
There was nothing to eat, but I felt too weak to go to
the store, and anyway, I didn't feel the least bit hungry.
My headache was so bad I could hardly think. I went
back to bed, but in the evening, still not feeling better, I
called the front desk. I was glad it was Tracy who picked
up, not one of the interns who sometimes filled in for
her. I told her my symptoms, and she said it sounded to
her like flu. "I get off in an hour, so I'll drop in on you."

A soft knocking awoke me. I got up to open the
door. When she saw me, Tracy laughed, she couldn't
help herself. "I'm sorry," she said, "it's just you look so
dreadful."

She had a whole arsenal of medicines with her, plus
sachets of chicken soup, rusks, and apple sauce in little
plastic pots. "Go back to bed," she said, "I'll fix you
some soup." The kettle droned. Tracy came to the side
of the bed, took my pulse and temperature. "A hundred
and four," she said, looking concerned. "Is that a lot?" I
asked. "Yes," said Tracy, "it is. But I won't be able to get
hold of a doctor at this time." She looked through her
supplies, plumped for one of them, and pressed a pill
out of its tin sheet. "Take one of these, they're supposed
to bring your temperature down."

I managed no more than a couple of swallows of
the soup. My throat was sore now too, and I really

didn't feel like eating. I lay there drowsily. I have
very dim recollections of that night. I can see Tracy
wandering around the room, she mops the sweat off my
brow, gives the bedding a shake, takes my temperature,
hands me another pill. She's sitting in the chair by
the fridge, telephoning. She's speaking so quietly, I
can't hear what she's saying. I don't know if she's got
a boyfriend or she's married with kids she needs to
take care of. I see a girl in a paddling pool with a little
toy boat in her hand, but I know that's a photograph
from Marcia's book. Tracy pulls the chair across from
the desk, sets it by the bed, sits down on it. She's got
Marcia's book in her hand. So you knew, she says. Or
am I imagining that? I did know, I recognized her.
Tracy opens the book, reads the dedication. She knew
it too. But was that Tracy? Or was it Marcia? Could it
have been Marcia the whole time, somehow ageless?
She lay in the bed beside me, stroking my brow, passing
me my tea. When she leans across me, her breasts
brush against my arm. You must drink something.
Those long-ago nights, when I was sick and my mother
sat by my bed, those precious hours of weakness and
being cared for.

Tracy is sick. Marcia is sitting at her bedside, lays
her hand on her brow, gives her a sip of tea. The camera
is on the bedside table. I step into the room. How is she

feeling? The fever's gone down slightly. She's asleep now. Marcia gets up, I can see from looking at her how tired she is. You go to bed, I'll stay up with her. I sit at Tracy's bedside, watch over her sleep, look at her unmoving face, for a thirtieth of a second, a sixtieth of a second.

Tracy is standing in the paddling pool we got her at Walmart and that only lasted for one summer, she's holding a toy boat in one hand, squealing with delight. Come out now, I say, your lips have gone blue. She splashes water at me. Careful of the camera, I hear Marcia's voice behind me. I bend down to pick Tracy out of the pool. Wait, says Marcia, and I hear the shutter click. Tracy is crying, her knee is bleeding. Get a bandage, says Marcia. I run inside, but this is a house I've never been inside, I don't know where the first-aid kit is, I start looking for it. What's keeping you? Marcia calls from the garden. Tracy is crying, howling, she's tiny, I can't believe how tiny she is. Her eyes are still shut, but her mouth is feeling for her mother's nipple. I am standing in the ward, looking around, where is the exit? There is no exit.

The sickness ended as suddenly as it began. I woke up one morning with a clear head and almost no pain. Sun was shining in through the window, and for the

first time I felt slightly at home in the studio where
I'd now been for over a month. I took a sip of the cold
tea that was on the bedside table, and was about to go
in the shower when there was a knock, and the door
opened a crack. "How are you feeling?" asked Tracy, but
she seemed to tell right away that I was doing better,
and she smiled broadly. "I'll fix you some fresh tea."

Not until I got up did I notice how enfeebled I still
was. Tracy helped me across to the little table. We sat
face-to-face, I with my tea, she with the mug of coffee
she'd arrived with. Once, she suddenly inhaled as
though to speak, but then she just smiled, and I smiled.
For the first time in our acquaintance I took a closer
look at her. She wasn't really striking in her casual
clothes, jeans and a shirt and a puffer vest with a little
horse's-head logo on it. Her hair was sensibly styled,
worn long but in a ponytail. She had little ear-clips and
a plain ring on her finger, probably a wedding ring. "Do
you have children?" I asked.

"Not yet," she said.

"But you are married?"

"Yes," said Tracy. "What about you?"

I shook my head. "Somehow it never happened."

We knew nothing about each other, and I think
at that moment we both understood it was too late to
make any amends for that.

"I'm glad you were here," said Tracy. "I'd better get back to work now."

All the following days, I steered clear of Tracy and didn't collect my mail, who knows why. I flicked through the book of Marcia's photographs, looked at the pictures long and hard, imagined a different life for myself, a perfect life for which it was now too late. I can't even say I regretted it, because I'd had an okay life so far, and couldn't really imagine living in some little burg in Vermont, hours from the nearest city and doing God knows what. I put the book down and got out my drawing things.

For the first time since I'd got here, I worked. It took me a while to find my rhythm, but after that it went well. I started taking meals with some of the other guests, and even got to know a few of them. I got to know Jeremy Muhn, whose show I had seen the night of my arrival. He looked nothing like the way I'd imagined a native American would look, he was tall and lean and so pale it looked like he never went out at all. He told me his material was roadkill, but just now there wasn't much of that around because of the snow. "If I could afford it, I'd rent a snowmobile," he said.

Jeremy had learned to treat cadavers from YouTube videos. One time I visited him in his studio, which looked and smelled like a lab. "No idea why I'm doing this," he said. "Hey, it's art."

I asked after his Native American forebears. He had a grandmother who was a Cowasuck, he said, but she hadn't known much about the culture either. As a young fellow, there was a time he'd been greatly interested in it, and he'd worked for a tribal organization and even tried to learn the language. "We are the children of the dawn, the men from the East. May the Great Spirit bless us." He laughed. By now, his ancestry didn't matter much to him. He had French blood too, and he didn't like Camembert. "I'm an American. We are whatever we can make of ourselves."

The big party was meant to take place just before Christmas, before everyone went home. But a few days before, the forecast turned bad, a blizzard was forecast, twenty inches of snow and temperatures well below freezing. Suddenly there was a commotion, everyone was afraid of getting stuck here and missing their family celebrations or some other important commitments. When I went walking in the morning, I saw people dragging their gear to the parking lot and stowing it away, hugging, exchanging addresses, last words. I went into reception, to collect my mail. There was quite a heap of it, but none of it mattered. Tracy was just booking a minibus to take a couple of foreign visitors to the airport at Burlington. We had a brief exchange, she asked me if everything was all right.

"I'm not going home till the New Year," I said. "I thought I'd spend a few days in New York."

She smiled. "Then I'm sure we'll see each other again."

On my way to the studio I ran into Jeremy. "Are you leaving?" I asked.

He shook his head and laughed. "I can't turn down free food." He said he lived somewhere fifty miles away, he'd get home one way or another. "Maybe my father'll pick me up." The first few snowflakes hung in the air. "Typical weather for the region," said Jeremy.

The big snow came exactly as predicted. The drifts of it deepened while you watched. The caretaker drove around all day with his snowblower, keeping the footpaths open, but as darkness fell, he gave up. The following morning, it was ankle-deep on the paths, and it was still snowing. After breakfast I went into the village. I had a book on order from Hilda and hoped to pick it up, but she said there hadn't been any deliveries yesterday. "I've visited the Alps," she said. "You Europeans aren't fazed by snow. Here, we just give in, stay home, and wait for it to melt."

Village life seemed to be in slow motion. Cars pushed through the snow at walking pace, and even the few walkers were slower than usual, putting their feet in holes in the deep snow, as though afraid of damaging it. Back at the foundation I saw Jeremy loading big cardboard boxes onto the back of a pickup. "This is my father," he said, putting his arm around the shoulder of a squat man who shook my hand. He didn't seem much older than me. We spoke briefly, then Jeremy's father said they'd better go, the roads weren't going to get any better. "You'll miss the Christmas party," I said to Jeremy. He shrugged his shoulders, then he too shook my hand. "Next time. May the Great Spirit be with you."

There was almost no one at lunch, and the mute girl cleared away nearly full dishes with an impassive expression. I had wanted to do a little more work, but I was distracted by the party and the prospect of meeting the benefactor and maybe even Marcia after thirty years. I ended up watching the weather channel all afternoon, following the satellite images of masses of damp air coming our way from the coast. In between there were little interview pieces with pizza delivery men or school-bus drivers; sometimes sad-seeming shots of snowbound roads and roofs or kids throwing snowballs or sledding. The weather people were boisterous, joking around and giving viewers tips for how to deal with the masses of snow. At nightfall the wind would swing around from northeast to northwest, they were saying, and freezing air from the Arctic would move into the interior. There would be no more precipitation and the mercury would plummet. I worked out the temperatures on my phone. They were predicting minus-twenty degrees Celsius.

The Christmas party was due to begin at six. I turned up punctually, but there was no one around. There were torches burning outside the benefactor's apartment and lights on in all the windows. I knocked and waited. I waited, then knocked again; when no one came I opened the door and walked in.

The large entrance hall was festively decked out in ribands and paper chains, with fir twigs and silver and golden baubles. There was no one there either, and I passed through a doorway into the living room, which was similarly decorated and also deserted. It was furnished with antiques, there were thick carpets on the floors, and blinds in the windows that looked as though they were never drawn. Altogether, for all its cozy decor, the room gave the impression of being unused, as though some decorator had rigged it up for a photo shoot. There was a gigantic Christmas tree in front of one window, so lavishly decorated you hardly saw anything green. At its foot were dozens of parcels wrapped in shining paper. On a large oval table were dishes and platters of food, elaborate canapés, filo pastries, all sorts of salads and pickles, whole salamis, sides of ham and roast beef and smoked salmon. There were even prawns and half-lobsters. In large chrome bowls, warmed by gas flames, there were meatballs in tomato sauce, sliced roast pork, dauphinoise potatoes, and vegetables. At one end of the table was a cheese board with all manner of cheeses, figs, pears, and grapes, and next to it a selection of desserts, pies and cookies, fruit salad and chocolate mousse and tiny handmade chocolates, some decorated with gold leaf. I looked at my watch, it was a quarter past six. After hesitating briefly, I went over to a second table and poured myself a glass of red wine. I sat down in one of the chairs that were placed along the wall but got up again right away, afraid of making a bad impression when the host appeared. On the walls were framed photographs, like the ones in my studio, evidently from the early days of the foundation. Over the fireplace hung a photograph I knew, it was the one of the Christmas party and the masked guests that was also in my studio. When I looked more closely at it, I saw that it had been taken in this very room. I could see the selfsame furniture and curtains, the Christmas tree in front of the same window, and right at the edge of the photo, a section of the buffet that seemed to be just as richly set as the one today.

I thought I could hear them, the guests from the past, their laughter and chatter. A woman squawked with laughter, someone began to sing a Christmas carol and stopped, flatware rattled on plates, somewhere a glass fell and broke. I turned around and saw the room full of people in costume. A man in a squirrel suit raised his glass to me, a woman in a classic black evening gown and a mask over her eyes pushed her arm through mine and led me in the direction of a group of men and women in bird masks, who nodded silently to me. The woman led me on across the room, as though following a prescribed route. The masked figures greeted me with a nod or a bow. A woman in a skintight striped suit and large zebra head curtseyed. Where is our host? I asked. Maybe he'll come later, said the woman, who smiled and pressed my arm. But it's already late, I said. Far too late, said the woman and she laughed as though she'd made a joke. I turned to her and gazed into her dark eyes glittering under the mask. Marcia? I hazarded. Much too late, she repeated, and led me back across the room under the same photograph on the hearth that I had just looked at, but now there was only the empty room, and a family group in front of the fireplace, a man and a woman and a couple of children, a slightly older girl and a small boy with a face that had something the matter with it. My handicapped little brother, said Marcia, letting go of my arm. When I turned, she was gone, and I was all alone.

I refilled my glass.

At seven there was still no one there, and I helped myself to more wine and finally went to the buffet. The food was delicious, but I wasn't hungry, and left my half-full plate on a coffee table. I poked at the parcels under the tree with my foot, but they seemed to be empty, dummies. I waited probably another hour and left. No one else had come.

It had stopped snowing and the sky was clear. It was freezing cold. There was no moon, just an endless number of stars. One trailed across the sky, but then I saw it was only an airplane. That same night, I packed my suitcase. As I was clearing up, I stumbled across the poetry volume I had found at Hilda's. I leafed through it again and reread the poem that reminded me of my story and Marcia's. The last lines went like this:

I have opened the doors
In sign of surrender. The house is filling with cold.
Why will you stay out there? I am ready to answer.
The doors are open. Why will you not come in?

I hesitated, then picked up a pencil, wrote "For Marcia" on the title page, and signed my name. At first I wanted to write my address as well, but then I thought the foundation had all my details anyway. If Marcia or Tracy wanted to get in touch, they would know how to find me. I laid the book on the table, closed my suitcase, and went to bed.

On the highway the traffic was backing up. By the time I got to the airport, it was dark. I gave back the car keys and took the subway into the city, getting out at Queens, the same stop I had lived near thirty-two years ago. I checked into a cheap hotel and from my room called the airline to rebook my flight. I was suddenly in a hurry to get home. All the Christmas flights were full, but they could squeeze me in on the twenty-sixth.

So now I have my few days in New York. There are some exhibitions I wouldn't mind going to. I could call the gallerist, but I don't think I will.

I don't mind being alone over Christmas. I will go to some good restaurants, take in a movie or two, maybe go for a walk, see if I can't find my old building, Marcia's old building. Something tells me they won't be there anymore, too much has changed in the meantime. My memories have paled and become indistinct. Probably I'll just go back to the hotel, watch TV, drink some whiskey, write a few texts or e-mails, get an early night. My life goes on.

Nahtigal

David had taken the mask with him, even though he wasn't planning on using it today—a squirrel mask that pulled down over his head. He had been given it as a birthday present years ago, long after he had stopped dressing up; perhaps because he was already at an age when he felt he was always dressing up anyway, even when he didn't want to be. His body felt to him like a badly fitting disguise, which turned his actual character and the thing he wanted to be, and thought he was, into something baggy and ugly. Why did it have to be a squirrel anyway, why not an owl or a wolf? He must have pointed it out to his mother sometime: Look, a squirrel, isn't it sweet? Then, years later, when she had no idea what to give him, she remembered, and—without thinking about it too much—bought it. David had worn it precisely once, on that birthday, and pretended to his mother to be thrilled with it. After that he had shoved it in the back of a drawer somewhere, shaming evidence of how little she knew him, how little anyone knew him. He peered into the plastic bag next to his chair and had to laugh at the use he was going to put it to now. His mother would be surprised—they all would be—at what her squirrel would get up to.

That morning, after she'd gone to work, David had called in sick. His immediate boss was on holiday, and the secretary didn't ask any questions when he said he didn't feel well. There wasn't much going on anyway during the summer, and the trainees were kept busy doing all kinds of silly make-work. Up in the storeroom there was an apparently endless supply of envelopes and receipt forms with the old telephone number on them, and when there was nothing else to do, the trainees would get together in the boardroom under the roof, where it was hot and airless, and paste little luminous stickers over them with the new number, which itself had been in use for years now. Most of the time, though, they were just messing about, either lethargic or high-spirited, or they hung around the coffee machine, or in one of the meeting rooms, always on the alert in case one of their superiors caught them idling.

David had intended to be in the city at ten, but after phoning the office he'd gone back to bed and fallen asleep—quite as if he was actually unwell. So it was ten-thirty by the time he was sitting outside the little café on the edge of town, looking across at the bank subbranch opposite, which was housed in a small single-family home. It was hot on the cobbled square, and the sun dazzled him. Since his arrival, no one had either walked in or out of the bank, only two women with bicycles had stopped for a chat on the pavement. The waitress came to take his order. She had to be sixty, but she was thin as a rail, in her skin-tight purple jeans. She opened out the sun umbrella over David's table, and asked him what he wanted. He ordered a latte. He had only started drinking coffee since becoming a trainee, not because he liked the taste, but because all the others did, and it seemed to be part of being a grown-up. He had only recently acquired a taste for alcohol too, though he only drank on company occasions, of which there was no shortage, office outings, summer parties, Christmas lunches, all kinds of things. David looked forward to these occasions, though they made him nervous as well.

Eleven twenty-three. A man in motorcycle gear and helmet walks into the bank, he jotted down in a small notebook he'd acquired and brought along for precisely this purpose. For a moment, he was afraid the man might have the same thing in mind as he did, and get in first. In suspense he waited till the biker came out again, settled himself unhurriedly on his machine, and rode away. The waitress had brought David his coffee and went over to the customers at the other table, two old men and an old woman with a small dog, who, in all the time David had been sitting there, had kept desultorily making conversation. Twice she had said goodbye already, and then failed to get up. Eleven thirty-four. Elderly couple enter the bank, David wrote in the notebook, and realized as he did so that he had forgotten to write down what time the man in biker gear had left. He was irritated by his absentmindedness; the least mistake could cause the entire undertaking to fail. Eleven thirty-six, he wrote, large Mercedes parks close to the bank, in front of a furniture store. A young woman gets out. She leans against the car, and seems to be waiting for someone.

There was a quote printed on the sugar packet. If thou art a man, admire those who attempt great things, even though they fail. Lucius Annaeus Seneca, 4 BCE–65 CE. David was still astonished at the way someone

like him, who wouldn't help himself to a cookie
without asking his mother's permission, had come upon
this plan. For weeks now, for months, he had been
thinking about it, imagined pulling the squirrel mask
over his head, walking into the bank and going up to
the counter. He pulled his father's army pistol from the
plastic bag, pointed it at the one customer in the bank,
and in a disguised voice, demanded the money from
the cashier. Money, he would say. All of it. Fast. He
had meant to practice disguising his voice at home, but
it made him feel so silly that he soon gave up.

Eleven thirty-nine. Couple leaves the bank. Young
woman walks up and down the pavement, smoking a
cigarette. David put his notebook away. The woman
seemed nervous. If the police questioned her, what
would she tell them? She wouldn't be able to furnish
them with a description of the young man, she
wouldn't even have noticed him going into the bank.
Only when the alarm went off would she have taken a
step in the direction of the bank, and then several the
other way. Then she would see him, a lean young man
in squirrel mask, jeans, and black T-shirt, getting on a
bike and disappearing around the corner.

David imagined himself driving the Merc down a
country road, the woman in the passenger seat, he laid
his hand on her knee and smiled. What's the plan? she

asked. France, he said, the Côte d'Azur. You're crazy,
she said, and laughed, I've brought nothing to wear.
Then we'll just have to buy you some new stuff, he said,
money no object. How much was there in his plastic
bag? A hundred g's? Two hundred? And what happened
when it was gone? They have banks on the Côte d'Azur
as well. You're crazy, she said again. You only live once,
said David, and put his foot down on the accelerator.
His first concern wasn't really money, it was taking
charge of his own life, being able to decide himself
what he did with it.

The young woman looked at her watch. David
looked at his. Ten to twelve. He mustn't stay here too
long, he didn't want the waitress and the other clients
to remember him when the police came around later,
asking about any suspicious individuals. He got up and
crossed the street. In the bank window was a table of
currency exchange rates, with Euros, US, Denmark,
UK, Norway, Sweden, Australia, Canada, Japan, all of
them countries where David had never been. And now
he remembered that he had forgotten to pay for his
coffee, and he ran back across the street. The waitress
seemed not to have noticed that he had gone.

The next day it rained. David went into the city
again. He had heard of bank robbers who scoped out
their prospective targets months in advance, took

down every detail, drew up plans of the building, took secret photographs of it. He sat in the bus, thinking what he still needed to do. Security cameras, he wrote in his notebook. Opening times. Counter room, escape route. He was so engrossed that he missed his stop, and got out the one after. Along one side of the street were small, rather decrepit-looking single-family homes, on the other was a large project with five-story apartment blocks from the fifties or sixties. Instead of heading back into town, David walked on out. The rain came softer, then harder. The road crossed a highway, and David leaned over the parapet of the bridge and watched the cars and trucks racing by below, and wondered where they were all going. How long did it take to get from here to the Côte d'Azur anyway? But he couldn't drive in any case, he had only turned eighteen a couple of months ago, and he couldn't afford a car, heck, he couldn't even afford driving lessons.

He left the main road and walked through side streets that led between the apartment blocks. In the covered entryway of one building stood a young woman smoking. In spite of the cool weather, she was just in jeans and a skimpy T-shirt; she seemed to be watching him. David looked the other way. This would be a good place to hide if I had to, he thought. He stopped and looked back. The woman was still looking his way, and on an impulse he went up to her. Her expression didn't alter, she looked at him with complete indifference. He asked if there was an apartment free somewhere here. The woman didn't reply, and finally said: Haven't you got an umbrella then? No, said David. You see, I'm looking for a place to live. Just for you? asked the woman. How old are you anyway? Her T-shirt was very light material, and David could see the lines of her bra through it. I'm not from here, he said. Nor am I, said the woman. A silence ensued, as though everything had been said, or nothing. Finally, the woman stamped out her cigarette and said, Well, bye, and turned away. It would be nice to live here, I reckon, said David. I don't think so, said the woman, and disappeared into the building without looking at him again. Through the glass door, David watched her go up the stairs. He hoped she felt his eyes on her and that she might turn and look his way. She would smile and go back downstairs, and let him in. Why don't you come in? It would be cool and a bit dark in her apartment. We should take off our wet things, she said. Even though hers weren't.

The tables were again out in front of the café, but the chairs had been folded away, and were stacked up against a wall. David stepped into the tiny interior that had no room for anything beyond a counter, a cigarette machine, and a couple of tables. The air was warm and

somehow heavy from the rain outside. At the table by
the entrance sat two old men and a woman with a little
dog, but different from yesterday's—it was as though
the same parts had been taken by different actors.
The waitress behind the bar was a different one too, a
plump woman of some indeterminate age. Could I get
a coffee? said David. The woman hesitated briefly, then
said, Yes, I think we have that. The other customers
laughed uproariously. That was a good one, said the
woman with the little dog.

David sat at the table at the back. There was a
crocheted window hanging, and he couldn't see the
bank from where he was, but it would have drawn
notice if he'd got up and left right away. He drank his
coffee in small sips and looked around. There were
postcards on the walls, no doubt sent by regulars here,
views of Ibiza, Bangkok, Kenya. On a barstool lay a
fluffy dog, the kind of thing you might win at a fair,
and on another a pile of cushions. On the bar was
a display for lottery tickets. Small price—big win. Is
today your lucky day? Win up to 250,000 right away.
When David left, he saw a hairdresser from the salon
next door drink an espresso outside. Clouds, he wrote
in his notebook, also the way all sounds seem to be
magnified by the wet surfaces, whether it's cars or
birdsong or church bells.

Back in the village, David headed straight home, he had to take care not to be seen by anyone from work. Once home, he turned on the TV, and ate the sandwiches he had made this morning for his lunch. In the afternoon he went out on his bike in the woods. He had the army pistol with him and wanted to try it out. He didn't have any ammunition, probably it wouldn't have been difficult getting hold of some, but it would have attracted attention and complicated matters. He stood in the middle of the woods and pulled the pistol out of the plastic bag, and in his disguised voice he repeated gruffly: Money. All of it. Right now. Money. All of it. Right now. The weather was due to improve on Thursday, Friday at the latest. Did that favor him? Was it easier to rob a bank in rain or shine?

This time David went a stop too far on purpose. More rain, he wrote in his notebook, and gusting wind. The middle of town smells like a pine forest. Feeling happy, a touch solemn, God knows why. It took him a while to find his way back to the tenement. There was no one around, and David read the names by the doorbells: Marra, Reisacher, Wittwer, Garofalo, Nahtigal. He settled on Nahtigal. And what was her first name? The first one that sprang into his head was Renata, he didn't know why. He didn't know anyone with that name. Renata Nahtigal, he said the name over a few times, wrote it in his little notebook. She didn't live here, she had said. Perhaps she was visiting her parents. David walked up and down the street, but she didn't appear. It started drizzling again, and he took shelter in the entryway where he had seen her the first time. You're all wet, said Renata, you'll catch cold. Her father was on vacation or in the hospital, she had come down to empty the letterbox, to water the plants. You can help me, she said, my father has a lot of plants. They sat on the sofa together, and Renata showed him snaps of her childhood. They sat huddled close, and the hand with which Renata was holding the album open was on David's thigh. You'd better be careful you don't get a cold, she said. Have you ever been to the Côte d'Azur? David asked.

It was noon. The trainees were sitting on benches in the town center, eating pack lunches or takeout. David looked at them and was envious of the placid rhythm of their daily life, which he had put at risk. They had good chances of getting ahead, of having a decent living like their parents and grandparents as a part of something bigger. He himself had been lost for such a life, even if he had shared in it up until a week ago. He couldn't put his finger on when he had realized there had to be a decision, it was as though he had only realized when it was too late. And everything that had happened or was yet to happen led him to this moment. He would stand outside the bank, take a couple of deep breaths, then pull the squirrel mask over his head and walk in and do what he had to do.

The secretary had called his mother and asked after David. What's the matter with you? his mother asked. You can't just call in sick and then go gadding about town. I really didn't feel well, said David. His mother laid her hand on his brow and said: Well, you're not running a temperature. And you're going in to work tomorrow. The day after, said David, it's not as though we were doing anything there anyway. His mother sighed and went into the kitchen to fix supper.

In bed, later, David went over every move he would make, every word he would say. He browsed through his notebook, read his notes. On the last page with writing, there was just the name, Renata Nahtigal. He turned out the light and tried to picture her face. At first he had thought she was his sort of age, but then when he stood in front of her, he saw from the fine lines in her face that she was older, maybe thirty or thirty-five. He went to the bathroom to take off his wet clothes. He took the plastic bag with him. Are you afraid I'll rob you? Renata called after him with a laugh. When he returned to the living room five minutes later, naked but for the squirrel mask over his head, she screamed, then her scream turned to laughter, and after that she couldn't stop laughing.

But that wasn't what he remembered thirty years later. It was that moment on the following day when he stood in front of the bank. Ten twenty-three. Two minutes earlier, an elderly woman had entered the branch, she would leave shortly. David stood there, holding in his hand a sports bag containing the squirrel mask and pistol. The weather had taken a turn for the better, but it was as though summer had broken over the two previous days of rain. The light had changed, the air was clearer, and there was a smell of autumn. A breeze was enough to make him shiver. He stood there, looked at his watch, ten twenty-four, took a couple of deep breaths. It felt like the moment on a swing when you're on top of the curve and are hanging there weightless for an instant, thinking you're on the point of taking flight, before gravity asserts itself and pulls you back into life.

The Most
Beautiful Dress

The first time I saw Felix, I had been working for him for several months, and had heard all sorts of stories about him. He was the George Clooney of dendrochronology, said Nicole, our boss, after their first meeting. Daniela, the project manager, also had the most amazing things to say about our chief archaeologist. During coffee breaks the two vied with one another to tell the most outrageous stories. Felix was incredibly good-looking, he was fit, well educated and intelligent, and a perfect gentleman. He goes swimming in the lake at lunchtime every day, said Daniela. She had a meeting with him and was wearing her bathing suit under her light summer dress. Are you going swimming with him? asked Nicole incredulously. In that case, I'll come too.

When they came back to the office at two, it turned out that things hadn't progressed beyond lunch. They were both a bit irritable. I wouldn't mind meeting him myself, I said. I hardly think that's necessary, said Nicole.

Then, two weeks later, I did meet Felix after all. I had finished the draft texts for the information boards that were going to be put up around the diggings, and because neither Nicole nor Daniela were around, the boss said I should take them around myself and talk them over with the chief archaeologist. He could give me his views in person. I called him, and we agreed to meet at eleven.

Hi, I'm Felix, he said, putting out his hand. He was tanned and was wearing a white plastic helmet, and I have to say he did look good. Brigitte, I said, I'm the graphic designer. If it was up to him, Felix said, then he wouldn't have all this onsite communication. We're here to dig. If it upsets people, we can't help it. He showed me into his office, which was in a shipping container, and I laid the folder in front of him on the table. He looked through the draft material without displaying much interest. Does the agency employ only women? he asked casually. No, I said, but all the women want to be working on this project. He looked up quickly and asked if it was because we were all so passionately interested in archaeology. Archaeologists, I'd say, and I smiled. He didn't seem to get it and closed the folder. You decide. You're the specialist. The *specialista*, I said, even though I wear my hair short. He looked at me and forced a smile. So you're interested in archaeology? The others couldn't make it, I said curtly, and could have smacked myself. Felix's cellphone rang and he took the call without speaking. As he listened, his expression darkened. It's the man in charge of the dig, he said, pocketing his phone. I've got to go down.

There were advanced plans for an underground parking area, but when traces of stilt houses were found, the construction was delayed by a year. A sheet of concrete—which later would be used as the roof of the carpark—was laid over the excavation, and let in it was a square opening, below which a metal staircase led down. Felix scuttled down the steps, and I followed him with the folder jammed under my arm. It was a warm day, and I was wearing sandals and had to take care not to slip on the metal steps. Felix got into some dispute with a squat little man with a ponytail and tattooed lower arms. An engineer was crouching in front of them, struggling with a big pump and cursing. I stopped just behind Felix. The other man stared at me unpleasantly and asked what I was doing there. I'm waiting for a decision, I said. Felix turned around and looked at me in annoyance. You can't come here dressed like that, he said, and took off his hard hat and draped it on my head, as though I was a child.

He introduced me to the man in charge of the excavation and said they were experiencing problems with the pump. If we didn't keep pumping water out, we could be doing our archaeology underwater.

He had a brief discussion with the head of the excavation, then waved me away, and I followed him down the vast hole to a group of young people who were squatting on the ground and scraping away a foot-deep layer of humus, using little trowels. Most of the stuff they just dropped behind them in a heap, but some small bits were carefully placed in cardboard boxes. I repeated that I needed a decision from him. This layer is around five thousand years old, said Felix. It's from the Neolithic period. He talked about pieces of material they had found, potsherds, bones and other food waste. The din from the drills was deafening, and there was a smell of exhaust fumes and damp earth. I picked up a scrap of blackened wood on the ground and asked if I could keep it. Why not, said Felix. What will you do with it? He said I had to put it in water when I got home, otherwise it would rot in no time. He walked on, then suddenly grabbed me by the arm and pulled me in with a quick movement. Watch out, he said. A digger passed close by me. This is where we found the skeleton, he said, under the layers of occupation. It was a young woman. She must have died over five thousand years ago. Maybe she fell in the lake and drowned. It was fascinating to listen to him, and slowly it dawned on me what Daniela and Nicole saw in him.

After about an hour, we went up again. My sandals were filthy, and my legs were splashed with mud. Well? I asked, did you decide which draft you wanted? You can be pretty obstinate, can't you? said Felix, and took the hard hat off my head.

He complimented me on my dress, said Nicole during our coffee break a couple of days later. The only females he's interested in are skeletons, said Daniela with irritation. In that case you're probably in with a good chance, aren't you? said the polygrapher with a grin. I asked if Felix had said anything about my designs. Nicole gestured dismissively. How do you like this: *You dig history? We dig it up.* Daniela pulled a face and left the kitchen. What's the matter with her? I asked. Nicole said she was probably upset that she had taken over the project.

A couple of weeks later, the boss said Felix had asked after me. He asked me where the little graphic designer was, he said, with a wink at me. I think Nicole schedules meetings with him deliberately on days when I'm not working.

Early in June, Felix sent a circular email to everyone involved with the project. They had collected some twenty thousand pieces of wood and processed ten thousand micro-sites, and wanted to celebrate with a little party tomorrow night. When I walked into the ladies' room at the end of the day, Nicole and Daniela were just getting themselves ready. Nicole was putting her hair up. She was wearing a dress of lime-green taffeta silk and heels. Daniela was got up like a princess as well. She looked me up and down and asked if I was going to the reception dressed as I was? I had just a simple cotton wrap dress and flats and next to the two of them I felt quite the ugly duckling.

I was about to leave when the boss called me in and gave me something that needed doing right away. By the time I got out of the agency, it was nine o'clock. I took the streetcar as far as the opera. The lakefront was full of nicely dressed people strutting up and down, all making an exhibition of themselves. I seemed to be the only one who was on my own. I had a strong sense of exclusion, and felt the stares of the men and the scowls of the women.

The baths where the reception was taking place was an old wooden construction set on piles out in the lake. When I saw it in front of me, I realized I wasn't in any sort of party mood. I sat down on the parapet of the quay. In the light of the setting sun, the opposite shore was nothing but a black outline. In the silvery glittering water I saw the heads of one or two evening swimmers. I had the sense I might as well be in the Stone Age. I had spent the day gathering berries and mushrooms on the wooded slopes of the Zurich Berg, then maybe I had woven cloth or ground corn. I felt sweaty, my back hurt, my hands were calloused. At the end of my long day, I had come down to the lake to swim in the light of the setting sun. I slipped off my shoes and undressed. A few passersby stopped and looked in astonishment as I got into the water stark naked, but it didn't bother me.

The cool water received me, and as I swam out, I suddenly felt the size of this mighty body that contained in its depths the history of millennia. I thought about the woman whose body had been found in the excavation; she had maybe struck out into the lake one summer evening, like me, and never made it back. The low sun was dazzling. When I turned away, I saw the stilted structure of the baths in front of me. The party guests had congregated on one of the wooden decks. I could hear them talking and laughing, the music and the noise from the nearby road, but all the sounds seemed to reach me from far away. I swam closer, and saw Felix standing by the wooden rails between Nicole and Daniela, looking out onto the lake. Nicole had her hand on Felix's shoulder, and seemed to be having an animated conversation with him. She looked quite lovely, and I felt a violent pang of jealousy that almost hurt me. I don't know what got into me when I swam a couple of strokes over to the stairs and climbed out of the water. It took a moment for the guests to notice me and turn in my direction. Conversations stopped, the shrill laughter of one woman died in her throat, then there was complete silence. Everyone was staring, recoiling from me as I made my way to the drinks table. I picked up a glass of chardonnay and toasted Felix, who was maybe ten feet away. Briefly I thought he wanted to say something, but then he mutely raised his glass. Although I felt perhaps more naked than at any time in my life, I had no sense of humiliation. It was a strange feeling of pride and sacrifice at once. This was about Felix and me, no one else, and the other guests in their glad rags were just extras, visitors from another era. I put the glass down untouched, walked over to the edge and dived in.

When I turned up the next day at break time, Nicole and Daniela were having a good old chinwag. They pretended not to have seen me. He drove me home, I heard Nicole whisper. And what was he like? asked Daniela. Nicole rolled her eyes. I got a coffee from the machine and went back to work. I felt like crying.

Just before twelve, I got an email from Felix. He said it was a pity I'd looked in so briefly last night. Did I feel like having supper with him? He wrote: You had the most beautiful dress. In a fury I wrote back to say he had obviously had a pretty good time without me, and I had a lot on my plate and no time to mess around. After that I heard nothing more from him.

Nicole and Daniela didn't refer to my appearance that evening, but they did treat me with more respect and distance. Nicole was different altogether after that evening. She was in a good mood and less impatient. And while it used to be that she stayed in the office after I left, she now regularly packed up at five, saying she had plans for the evening.

In the summer I went to Australia for a month and attended a language school. When I got back, the excavation work at the opera was over, and we had new contractors.

One evening in September I was standing around downstairs when the excavation boss walked in. Once again, his unpleasant look struck me. I wondered what he was doing here. While I spoke to the secretary, Nicole appeared and kissed and hugged him like a young thing. I wonder how long that'll work for, said the secretary, as we watched the couple leave. Did you catch his wandering eyes?

The following day, I asked Nicole about her new boyfriend. I thought you and Felix were an item, I said. She shook her head. That was done after your appearance at the party. You were a bit underdressed, wouldn't you say?

I thought of calling Felix, but what could I say? There wasn't anything between us, and I was ashamed of my jealousy. Anyway, I doubted whether he was seriously interested in me. If he had been, he wouldn't have given up so quickly, he would have written to me again. Just the same, I started going to the baths at lunchtime, in the hope of perhaps running into him. There were two decks surrounded by changing rooms, one for women, one for men, and between them, right at the entrance, an area for both sexes. Most of the time, I sat in the café there, so as not to miss Felix, in case he showed. He didn't.

I went to the baths in all weathers. If it was raining or gloomy and there was no one else there except me, I still got changed and wandered over to the men's deck, which happened to be where the party had been held that time. I sat down on the boards, dangled my legs, and looked out into the gray lake.

It was on one of the last days before they closed the baths for winter. It had been gray for days. There was a light drizzle coming down, and the towel I wrapped myself in was sodden. Again, I was thinking about the Stone Age builders who had frozen in their huts right here, five thousand years ago. They must have worried if they had enough food to get them through the winter, if the snow would come early and make it impossible for them to collect firewood. They must have been terrified of illnesses, accidents, wild beasts. And suddenly I felt a great sense of freedom, and it seemed ridiculous to be waiting for a man I barely knew, with whom I had spoken once, and who had treated me like a child.

From the shore, I heard the church clocks strike one. I was about to get up when I felt a hand on my shoulder. In alarm, I spun around and saw Felix standing behind me. He was in bathing trunks and had a towel over his shoulders, and he was smiling. I've been expecting you, I said. Me too, he said, as he helped me up. Then, without another word between us, we fell into each other's arms as though we'd been waiting five thousand years to do so.

Supermoon

'm sure they didn't mean any harm by it, they were in
the elevator, chatting, and they just didn't notice me.
I even had the sense that someone made a move for
the open button as the doors were closing, or at least
made as if to move for the button, as though he had
seen me, and wanted to let me in, before noticing he'd
left it too late. But maybe I was just imagining that. So
what, they didn't see me, it happens. Even though I was
standing in the middle of the doorway.

I would have a hard time explaining the nature of
our work to someone on the outside. It has to do with
the maintenance of civil aircraft. A plane is made up

of several million parts, and each one carries a number and a set life expectancy. Each time a plane is serviced, some parts need to be replaced and others inspected and, if necessary, replaced. Some are taken out and put back in again, to be replaced at the next servicing, or the one after. In addition to the mechanics and engineers, the maintenance people, the welders and painters and electricians and all the other specialists involved, there are also us office workers, a small army of employees whose job is seeing that everything is done according to plan and nothing is forgotten. Of course, the work has long since been computerized, but a lot of the programs are antiquated and written in software that hardly anyone can still work with. For years they've been talking about reprogramming everything, which would of course simplify things enormously, but because the job is so complicated and everything is bound up with everything else, no one dares to change anything, for fear the entire system could crash.

I am one of this small army of employees, who keep it all going; basically, I'm responsible for a list of items. It might not sound like much, but it's a long and very important list. I am a part in a complex system, I too have been given a number and a set life expectancy, at the end of which I will be swapped out and go into

retirement. I can't say I'm particularly looking forward
to it, but I accept the need for it, it's best for the firm,
and hence best for me too.

Our open-plan office is on the second floor of an
administrative building, with views of a small clump
of trees and the highway, the B-road running parallel
to it, and a railway line. We used to be in an office
with a view of hangars and tarmac, but I'm not sorry
we moved to the north side a few years ago, where the
summer temperatures are a little more bearable. I get
out to the hangars often enough anyway, either in the
course of my work or else in the evening when I stroll
over there, to exchange a few words with the people in
quality control or the warehouseman who issues the
tools and is responsible for seeing that none of them
is left inside the plane when the procedure is finished.
It's always a big moment, when one of those huge
machines rolls out of the hangar, ready for new flights
to distant lands. We may not wear smart uniforms
here like the flight crews, but in the end our job is just
as important as theirs, even if most of the passengers
aren't even aware of our existence.

There are five of us in the office, each with his own
special area, which the others don't know much about,
just whatever he or she happens to have been told. No
one says anything about the business with the elevator,

and I decide not to raise it either. I start up the desktop and read the emails that have come in since last night—there aren't as many as there usually are, but I'm not about to be out of work. A not inconsiderable part of it consists of the responsibility I bear, whether I'm working on the list or otherwise. I guarantee its rightness and up-to-dateness, which means sometimes more effort, sometimes less.

Is anyone going for lunch? I have to repeat the question, until Walter says he has an engagement. Gabi? She's staring at her screen. Gabi? At last she seems to have heard. Do you fancy some lunch? She needs to finish an email she's writing, I think her work has something to do with kerosene purchases.

We join a couple of colleagues from preservicing. They are discussing the new overtime rules. Gabi joins in, and the discussion gets a little testy. I don't get involved, I'm only here for a couple more days anyway, the new rules won't affect me. Besides, I haven't done any overtime for years. On the contrary, I've had to take care not to work too fast and be sure to fill up the hours, in case the boss got any ideas. The feeling at table is irritable. Eventually, everyone simply gets up and goes back to their desks without saying bye. I trot along after Gabi. She ignores me, as though I was the one she had been having an argument with.

We were a generation raised to offer an elderly person our seat on the bus or train, or at the very least to lift our bag onto the luggage rack, so that we didn't occupy both seats. Excuse me, is this place taken? The young man is wearing headphones, but his music is so loud I can hear it even in the moving train. I tap him on the shoulder. He jumps and looks at me in alarm. Is this place taken? He continues to look perplexed, but finally puts his bag up, and I get a seat.

On the way home from the bus stop I spend a long time waiting at the crossing. Pedestrians have priority, but you'd be amazed how few motorists accept that. Years ago, the residents' association petitioned the town council for a set of lights, but we were told it was too expensive and not necessary. Since then, traffic has only gotten worse, but no one talks about putting in traffic lights anymore. Today I don't get annoyed, and I wait patiently for a gap in the traffic. It's one of the first warm days of the year, almost springlike, even though we're still in February.

Hedwig seems not to have heard the door open. When I walk into the living room she gives a start. Then she smiles with relief. Oh, it's you. As though it could be anyone else, suddenly appearing in our apartment. I brush her a kiss, she briefly looks up from her book and goes back to reading. I flick through the evening paper. Hedwig makes no move to go to the kitchen. When I ask her what there is for supper, she says she doesn't really feel hungry, and she reads on. This has never happened in all the time we've been married, which is forty years. But I am, I say, and I laugh. Hedwig offers no reaction. I don't know what it is she's reading, but it seems to have gotten her whole attention. I go in the kitchen and fix myself a sandwich. I'm not that hungry either, truth to tell.

Later, I switch on the TV; Hedwig is still reading. Eventually she leaves the room. I thought she might have popped out to the bathroom. When she fails to come back, I go looking for her, only to find her already asleep in bed. She didn't even wish me a good night.

The following morning, I have a job waking her. Usually she's the early riser, and I can smell coffee when I wake up, but today she's still fast asleep. Perhaps the sudden break in the weather has made her tired. When I touch her on the shoulder, she opens her eyes and looks at me sleepily. Oh, you, she says. Don't get up, I say, feeling sorry I've woken her, have a lie-in.

Something funny happens on the way in to work. A young woman fiddling around with her phone almost sits down in my lap. She's practically on top of me before noticing there's someone sitting there, and she jumps up with a shock. Had I been younger, I might have said, Go ahead, don't mind me, but these days you can't say that sort of thing. Instead, I apologize to her, as though it was me that had been careless.

There are no emails today, and nothing in the internal mail either. Presumably, people are already taking their questions to my successor, even though I haven't handed over to him yet. Strictly speaking, Dieter's not my successor either, he's been working in the department for some time already, I'm not exactly sure what his field is. Anyway, it seems he's been deputed to look after the items on my list, in addition to whatever his previous line was. I warned the boss that he's underestimating the labor involved in the upkeep of the list, the number of changes that need to be made daily, but he just shrugged his shoulders and remarked, I'm sure Dieter will manage. I shoot him an email, asking him to phone me so that we can fix a time for the handover. He hasn't replied by noon. Then I happen to see that my email came back. *Delivery to the following recipients failed permanently.* And the reason: *Unknown user.* Even though we must have exchanged dozens of emails.

At lunchtime, everyone goes off, without anyone asking me to join them. I must say, they could have been a bit nicer to me on my last days. I have always tried to be a good colleague. I may not be a barrel of laughs, but I've always been loyal and dependable.

There's a squirrel leaping about in the trees outside the window. I watch it for a long time jumping from branch to branch, as though immune to gravity. Then a second one appears on the scene, and a wild pursuit begins, spiraling up and down, round and round the trunk. I'm not really hungry anyway.

I wonder if my colleagues have been suddenly struck with deafness. I need to say everything two or three times before anyone responds. The oddest thing, though, is that I can only hear it dimly myself, as though I had on a set of ear protectors, specifically to tune out my own voice. All other sounds I register clearly and distinctly, if anything they seem even a little louder than normal, as though I were hearing them through some kind of acoustic magnifying glass, if there could be such a thing. The second email I sent Dieter hasn't come back. I'm sure he'll get in touch tomorrow.

I go home a little earlier than normal, after all I didn't take my lunch hour. And I don't really know what to do with myself, there's not much point in embarking on something new with Dieter due to take over next week anyway, he's bound to have his own way of doing things. On the train I stay out in the corridor, afraid of provoking the sort of incident that happened this morning. I kept thinking about that all day. In retrospect, it seems less amusing than peculiar.

I watch a man tapping around on his phone with an expression of engaging in some life-or-death communication. He briefly looks up, seeming to have sensed me looking at him, then goes back to his frantic tapping. When he gets out at the next station, without taking an eye off his gadget, I see that he's been playing a computer game. He stops on the platform, still playing, while the train moves off.

Hedwig is not at home. There is nothing entered on the kitchen calendar, and I can't remember her saying anything about a call or engagement anywhere. The fridge is almost empty. I go to the nearby grocery store and buy bread, butter, salami. There's no one else in the store. There's a bell next to the cash register, but I never liked to use it, it seems impolite to me to ring for the cashier—like whistling to a dog. After a couple of minutes in which no one comes, I give it a shake, and a little later, another. Finally, I pack up my purchases, I'll pay when I'm next in the store. There've been times when I didn't have my wallet on me, and the owner said to me, That's all right, you can pay me tomorrow. On my way home, it briefly crosses my mind not to pay at all. After all, it's not my fault if no one's there. But then I remember that the store has video surveillance. The idea of being convicted of shoplifting after so many years amuses me, I couldn't say why. Perhaps it's the notion of having a dark side, unbeknown to anyone, and doing things no one would imagine me capable of. But I have no other side; I am, so to speak, a one-sided individual.

I can barely manage to unlock the door. When I locked it half an hour ago upon leaving, it seemed to be working normally, but now the lock is jammed.

I put my purchases away in the kitchen. I don't feel hungry now, maybe I'll eat something later on. Hedwig still hasn't come home yet, but for some reason I'm not worried about her, it's not so much faith as indifference. As I read the paper, I find myself scanning most of the articles, nothing seems to really concern me, nothing holds me. But then a word jumps out at me, there's an article about the so-called supermoon. At no time in this year has the moon been so close to the earth as on the next few nights, it has never been so bright.

Normally, I don't have any trouble getting off to sleep, but tonight I lie awake for a long time. I'm not worrying about Hedwig, but I feel like I'm staring into a vast space with eyes shut. I don't have any sensation, I don't even feel tired. It's not an unpleasant feeling, just an unfamiliar one.

The next morning, I feel a bit feeble, but that's hardly surprising as I've eaten nothing and barely slept for twenty-four hours. Even though I still don't feel hungry, I take a yogurt out of the fridge. When I've finished it, I can't decide to throw the empty container in the trash—it's as though that would be a decision of far-reaching consequences. As I brush my teeth, I find it difficult to get a clear sight of myself in the bathroom mirror. My eyes are pretty good for my age, but I can only see a blurred outline. Even after rinsing my eyes in cold water, it doesn't improve.

When I lock the door to the apartment, I realize that my trouble has nothing to do with the lock being stiff, it's simply that I don't have the strength to grip and turn the key properly. On the staircase I have to hold on to the banister because my legs feel like jelly.

The bus is almost empty, the train too. I hesitate briefly before going into the carriage. I'm tired, but have a great feeling of lightness, almost weightlessness. The light that comes into the compartment seems painfully bright, the shadows cast by the passing trees make it flicker like a stroboscope. I still feel sick, and I'm relieved when my station comes and I get out. At least my vision has gotten better.

There is hardly anyone around. It's only at the door that I realize that it's a Saturday. In all those years, this has never happened to me before. Even so I go up to the office, sit down at my desk, and switch on the computer. The squirrel is performing again on the trees outside, and I watch. I have the feeling I'm just as light as that creature, and that I too could leap around the trees like that. Once someone asked me what kind of animal I'd be if I could, I don't remember who it was, but I do remember I didn't have an answer. Why not a squirrel?

Around twelve I leave the office without having done anything. I take the train back, and then the bus. I buy what I need and stand in line at the checkout counter. In front of me is a woman I've seen before, but I don't remember her name. She doesn't seem to have noticed me anyway. When it's my turn, the cashier gets up and walks over to the shelves and starts stacking something. Hey, can I pay? I say. She doesn't seem to hear. I pack my purchases in a bag and leave.

Even though I've hardly bought a lot, the bag after a couple of hundred yards feels very heavy, and I set it down on the pavement briefly and catch my breath. When I bend down to pick it up again, it feels even heavier. I leave it there, after all, the fridge is full of the things I bought yesterday, and I don't seem to be hungry in any case.

The lock this time is too much. I can't grip the key, which keeps slipping through my fingers. I suppose I ought to be worried, but I'm not. On the contrary, I feel a strange levity. I flop down on the stairs and lean my head against the wall. Downstairs, I hear the front door open, and someone coming up the stairs. It's the woman who lives on the floor above us, but I can't remember her name even though we've been neighbors for many years. She passes me by without saying hello, without even acknowledging my presence. A few more people pass up and down the stairs that afternoon, they all look familiar, but no one seems to notice me. One time, I need to pull in my legs, afraid that one of the children running down the stairs will trip over me and fall.

I'm thinking about my list and wondering if it really was as important as I always believed. Every day I made changes to it, deleting some files and adding others, but I don't know who really needs it, and who else has access to it. All I know is that it's printed out every month and sent by the company mail to a dozen departments. I have seen it, thick volumes of lined computer paper gradually yellowing on the shelves, and removed after a certain length of time. I never dared ask whether anyone consults the list, perhaps because

I've long sensed that they don't. But sometime someone determined all these processes, and there must have been a reason, why else should so much paper be bound and mailed? Maybe it's not a matter of anyone needing the information on the list. Like everything else, they are just a part of reality, and their existence doesn't need any justification. The list is there, as much as we are, and that will have to do.

I have no idea what the time is when Hedwig finally gets home. She looks exhausted. She doesn't seem to see me either. I am on the point of moving aside to let her pass, but she walks right through me. She dumps her full shopping bags in the kitchen before coming back to lock the door. I took advantage of the moment to slip inside. After that, I'm so exhausted that I remain seated in the corridor. I am glad Hedwig hasn't turned the light on, my eyes are unusually sensitive, my hearing likewise. Although the kitchen door is closed, I can hear every word the man says on the radio, hear overdistinctly Hedwig chopping onions, opening and closing the fridge, I hear the bubbling of the kettle, the clatter of pans, and even the gas hissing out of the stove, the clicking of the lighter, the flicker of the flame.

I don't have the feeling that Hedwig is missing anything, that she misses me. She has cooked her supper, taken it into the sitting room, and sat down. She hasn't set a place for me, and I can feel no unrest in her movements, no expectation. I don't know why I can see all this. I haven't moved in all this time, but it's as though my consciousness could float around freely in the apartment, as though I could see and hear everything, as though I was everywhere and nowhere at once. Only in the corridor, where a moment ago I sat down, there seems to be some sort of concentration, a shapeless darkness.

I try to speak, but I don't succeed. The feeling of being at once very heavy and very light, immobile and floating, is an exhausting one.

Hedwig eats slowly and carefully. She wipes her mouth on a paper napkin, clears her throat, carries the dirty plates into the kitchen. She cleans the kitchen, washes the dishes, opens the window to let fresh air in.

I feel the chilly air streaming in, seizing hold of me and bearing me across to the window. I try to hold on somewhere, but I can't, I have no arms, no legs, no sort of body.

The moon is full and it really does seem brighter than usual and very close. It's as though it were drawing me up to it. The stars too are so bright that they seem to tremble. I climb slowly up into the air, see our building dwindle, see our little street, then the main road, with no traffic on it just now, our part of town, then the whole city. The moonlight is very bright, the scenery is easy to discern. I climb and climb. The lake, the hills in the distance, the snow-covered mountains. Before long I will see the Mediterranean, and then Africa, the Atlantic, America. I climb.

Sabrina, 2019

The first time Sabrina saw herself she was a little startled. She knew what she was letting herself in for, Hubert had explained it to her, and she had given her agreement, more than agreement, she was pretty enthusiastic about his idea. The fact that he had asked her of all people had flattered her and made her happy for a whole day. When he said he was looking for a model, she'd been apprehensive at first, in case he was one of those people who take erotic photographs of underage girls, but she'd heard him out, and so learned that it was nothing like that at all, and that he was a serious artist. She was happy to cooperate, even though she had no interest in art, or perhaps no understanding of it. He had explained lots of technical matters to her, the whole process, but by then she had switched off, that was all his business, all she needed to do was look pretty. Then she'd visited a museum to look at sculptures. She examined them carefully, imagined standing in their midst, herself a sculpture. She copied the poses, till she noticed a museum guard watching her; that gave Sabrina a pleasant sense of superiority. She was going to be a servant of the art, and that was something noble and significant.

Hubert had asked her to bring clothes she felt comfortable in, everyday sort of things. Her little wheeled suitcase contained a couple of classier outfits, things she might wear for a night out with her girlfriends, but after to-ing and fro-ing a little bit, he had plumped for a pair of ripped low-rise jeans, a crop top, and sneakers. Each time she got changed, he turned his back, which she thought was sweet but not really necessary. She wasn't inhibited, and was used to all kinds of things from her job in the hospital. The scanner, which looked like a large iron, threw a web of light across her body, and she was put in mind of the patients she escorted to have their MRIs or X-rays taken. For a moment she wondered if Hubert could see inside her with that machine of his, and see things about her that she wasn't even aware of, such things as illnesses, destiny, secrets.

So now she was confronting herself, only this second Sabrina wasn't flesh and blood but aluminum, and an inch or so bigger, which made her appear somehow threatening. The fact that next to the sculpture was a second, identical copy also had its disquieting aspect. Sabrina inspected her image, if anything, more carefully than she'd ever looked at herself. She could see herself at angles that her mirror didn't offer, from behind, from the side. She got down on her haunches and looked up at herself, she stepped away and moved back in, she went right up to one of the figures. Her earlobes suddenly struck her as tiny, and the ears themselves were just weird with all their windings and swellings. She didn't like her posture either, standing there with outthrust pelvis and bare belly. She caught herself standing there in that same way, pushing her belly out at the sculpture, as though in a contest. She lifted her T-shirt to show the other Sabrina the navel-piercing she still wore, the hand of Fatima, an Islamic emblem that was meant to keep evil spirits away, as one of the doctors had recently told her. Sabrina had just taken a liking to the figure of the little hand in the store, and got the piercing done, without thinking about it much. Around her neck, metal Sabrina was wearing a gold chain, just like, and the jeans copied every seam and crease, the precision of it was a bit baffling, almost scary.

Well, and how do you like yourself? asked Hubert, who had sent her on ahead, because he still had something to discuss with the metal caster. She wondered if Hubert considered her attractive. She was certainly not plain-looking, but she wasn't strikingly beautiful either, she couldn't kid herself. Once, when she was still a girl she had asked her mother if she thought she was nice-looking, the mere question had humiliated her, regardless of what her mother had replied. But beauty didn't seem to be Hubert's criterion. To go by the other work of his that he had shown her, she wouldn't have been able to tell his type, whether he liked women with slim or full figures, with hard or soft features, long or short hair. He was looking for perfectly ordinary-looking women, he had told her the first time they met, and then straightaway apologized and said something nonsensical about all women being beautiful of course. She had found that more offensive than comforting. When she had gone to his studio, he had given her coffee and showed her pictures of other sculptures, and a book about Pompeii with photographs

of plaster casts of the victims. A man trying to shield
the face of his pregnant wife with the corner of his
garment, to protect her from the falling ash, a woman
holding her baby in her arms, fleeing an ineluctable
death. This is morbid, said Sabrina. I find it fascinating,
said Hubert. They're all long dead, of course, but this
gives them a chance for us to look at them. I don't
think that's right, said Sabrina, at least I was asked if I
wanted to be a model.

How many clones of me are you going to make
anyway? she asked. Five or six, said Hubert, it all
depends on how well they sell. Will you give me one?
Sabrina knew from his expression that her request
was inappropriate. He had told her how expensive
they were to make, and her own contribution to the
project was fairly negligible. She had put her body at
his disposal for a day, had tried out a few costumes
and poses, and then maybe stood still for a couple of
hours while being scanned, but that was it. There were
endless women who could have done it and done it just
as happily and willingly as she did.

I'm not really serious, she said. What would I do
with something like that anyway? Put it in the sitting
room in my co-op? Use it for a clothes stand? But it was
too big to fit her clothes. How much do they weigh?
she asked and tapped the sculpture with her fingernail.

Don't touch, please, said Hubert. Maybe seventy or eighty pounds. Sabrina laughed. So you've made a taller and skinnier version of me. Or not skinnier, just lighter, I suppose, she said, pulling a face. When they said goodbye, they shook hands. Was that it, then? she asked, in some disappointment. You can come to the private view, he said, fishing a card out of his briefcase.

Sabrina had never been to a private view and felt immediately out of place. She was far and away the youngest person there. Hubert had called her just ahead of time, and said he thought it might be fun if she came in the same clothes she had worn for the sculpture, and now she felt wretched in the old stuff. The other women wore makeup and were in smart clothes and all looked very confident and somehow radiated importance. Most people seemed to know one another, and they exchanged greetings and laughed a lot. If Sabrina had only had someone with her, but her girlfriends all had better things to do. She picked up a glass of chardonnay and strolled through the show, only taking pains to avoid her own image, she really didn't feel like being identified by someone and spoken to. The thing with wearing the same clothes was an awful idea, and she was furious with Hubert, also because of the way he'd just given her a cursory greeting and then left her standing there while he went off to talk to more important people, people who had money and understood art, the kind of people who belonged here. The figure might bear Sabrina's name, but she herself was perfectly exchangeable.

When the gallery owner stopped everything and gave a little speech, Sabrina was already onto her third glass. She could feel the alcohol getting to her, but at least she didn't feel as out of place as she had when she'd arrived. The gallery owner welcomed everyone and then said a few words about Hubert and his new work. Most of what he said went in one ear and out the other. When he said of the sculpture, *Sabrina 2019*, that she looked out of place in the exhibition space, he might have said the same thing about her. He talked about the loneliness of the sculpture, her solitariness. Hubert wasn't concerned with a true-to-life mimesis, all his works were an expression of his strong feeling and thinking. Sabrina wondered what the feeling might have been in their case—it certainly wasn't anything concerning her. Don't you wonder what this seemingly randomly chosen girl is thinking, looking out at the world with that quizzical expression? the gallery owner mused aloud. Then he paused briefly and went on to the next piece. So she was now a randomly chosen girl with a puzzled expression. Ideally, she would have vanished straightaway, but something kept her there, she didn't know what it was herself. She took another glass of wine and texted her girlfriends: what was keeping them?

I've just bought you, said a voice in her ear, making her jump out of her skin. She looked up from her phone and saw a man of sixty or so whom she had noticed earlier because he seemed so confident in the way he negotiated the room, saying hello to right and left, as though he lived there. She had seen Hubert— looking smaller than he sometimes did—having a lengthy conversation with him. The man held out his hand: Robert Lang. Sabrina, she said. I know, he said, Sabrina, 2019. He laughed, but not unpleasantly. I hope you won't mind the fact that you'll be standing in my house before long. I never imagined anyone would buy her, said Sabrina. But of course, silly, Hubert has to live off something. Live pretty well too, I should say, said this Robert Lang, with another laugh. Do you have any idea how much you're costing me? Not me, said Sabrina, that tin girl is, I don't get a penny. She was half-irked, half-flattered by the man's interest. I couldn't begin to afford her. Well, you have only to look in the mirror, said the collector. But if you feel like it, why not pay yourself a visit? He gave her his card.

Later, when Sabrina told her friends in the hospital about the conversation, they were unanimous in saying the man was after something. He's not paying tens of thousands of francs for your statue if he doesn't want something from you, said Jasmin, and Tamara said, maybe he's one of those pervy men that has sex with statues. How do you get that? asked Sabrina. She's made of aluminum. Tamara said she wasn't sure either, but there was something she'd seen once on YouTube. You're crazy, said Sabrina, anyway, he's ancient.

The next day, after work, Sabrina went to the gallery again. There was no one there except a young woman looking pretty and bored at a desk. If she hadn't happened to have her phone out, whispering something, one might have supposed she too was a work of art. This time, Sabrina made a beeline for her sculpture. She looked different from yesterday, a bit smaller, and her expression looked somehow disappointed, or melancholy. Sabrina laid her hand on her bare upper arm and felt the chilly metal. Take it easy, girl, she said quietly, he won't do anything to hurt you. He seemed quite nice, really. She sat down on a bench along the wall, and stayed there awhile, not looking at the sculpture, she simply felt the need to keep herself company. For once, she managed not to pull out her cell right away, to send a text or watch a video or play a game. She just sat there as still as her image. What do you think, she asked herself, should I get the piercing taken out? It's a bit of a pain, and in winter no one sees it anyway. Or do you need protection from evil spirits? Shall we grow our hair out? Or get it all chopped off? It might be time to toss that old top, it's really not a nice color anymore. You doing all right? Mom's a pain, but you knew that. Calling all the time. And of course co-op life's not as cool as I'd hoped. Still, better than hanging around at home. But you—you're moving somewhere swank, I've heard. Maybe he owns some more sculptures, so you'll have a bit of company.

After a while the receptionist came over from her desk and asked if she could help in any way. That's me, said Sabrina, with a nod in the direction of the sculpture. So it is, said the young woman, laughing. Would you like a coffee? Sabrina shook her head. No, I just wanted to spend some time with her, that's all.

Sabrina's phone beeped, she had a text message. It was Jasmin, asking about going out tonight, Tamara was coming and the Finnish intern and one of his friends. Sabrina resented the interruption, and all the more when half an hour later Jasmin sent her a follow-up message. Leave me alone, won't you? muttered Sabrina, and turned off her phone.

Shortly before five, the girl from reception came over to her again and told her the gallery was about to close. Out on the street Sabrina suddenly burst into tears and felt utterly ridiculous.

As long as the show was on, Sabrina went to the gallery almost every day, sometimes on her lunch breaks, or before or after work, depending on her shift. Most of the time there was only the girl there. To begin with, she'd been a bit snooty, but over time she had gotten accustomed to Sabrina, and if there were no other visitors and she had no other work, she sometimes sat with her and chatted. Her name was Alexandra and she'd studied art history, it was her dream to work in a museum and be a curator. Sabrina had to ask what that was. Usually, she just listened to her, she didn't have much to say herself to interest Alexandra, hospital tidbits, which assistant doctor had hauled her over the coals today, catching a patient smoking in the closet, a man with dementia pinching her bottom, the trivia that made up her day.

When Jasmin or Tamara asked her at such times to come out with them to the cinema or a bar or disco, she would always refuse. The pair of them were annoying her more and more, their chitchat and banter, their silly talk and their way of lusting after the doctors and the Finnish intern. Haven't you anything better to do? she asked once, and stalked out of the staff canteen. Her roommates in the co-op were getting on her wick as well.

On one of Sabrina's visits to the gallery, Alexandra said she would never have agreed to serve as a model herself, and then straightaway apologized, saying she didn't mean it in a critical way. It's just that I can't imagine being immortalized in that way. I think you look great, said Sabrina, you would make a lovely sculpture. Then she asked Alexandra if she had ever heard anything about people having sex with statues. Alexandra's eyebrows shot up. Do you think, Sabrina went on hesitatingly, do you think the man who bought the statue of me...? Alexandra laughed out loud. Robert Lang? No, absolutely not. He's an important collector who's already bought several other works of Hubert's. It has nothing to do with you. But he said I should visit him if I liked, said Sabrina. I'm sure he only did that as a courtesy, said Alexandra. Would you take him up on it? Alexandra hesitated. Then she said: He has an amazing house, with a pool.

It was strange, but suddenly Sabrina envied her silvery double the chance to live in a beautiful house, remote from the unpleasantnesses of daily life, irritable doctors who were short with you, and irritating colleagues and crowded streetcars. It felt to her as though the statue was occupying the place that should have been hers.

You need to think about saying goodbye to your sister, said Alexandra. It was early October. Sabrina had quite forgotten that the exhibition was almost over, her visits to the gallery had become part of her daily routine in the past month. She's not my sister, she said, I'm an only child. It's me. Alexandra shrugged. Anyway, Saturday is the closing, do you want to come? Hubert will be there, and I'm sure the buyer will as well.

This time, Sabrina got dolled up, she put on her prettiest dress, made up her face and painted her nails—fingers and toes—with the pale blue nail varnish that Jasmin had given her for her birthday. But Robert Lang wasn't there, he was in Japan, the gallery owner said, when Sabrina asked him. He was a little curt with her, and Alexandra seemed distracted

and less friendly than usual. Hubert seemed surprised
to see Sabrina, evidently no one had told him of
her frequent visits. He seemed a little irritated when
she told him, and about the feelings she was now
having for the sculpture. The fact that she started
crying didn't help either. Listen, said Hubert, I can
understand it's something special for you, but for me
it's the most normal thing in the world. The history of
art is full of unknown models, men and women who
earned a bit of pin money by standing still and being
painted or molded. Earlier, it would have been much
more strenuous than it was for you, it meant standing
around for days on end in badly heated studios. But
you didn't pay me any money, said Sabrina. And she
has my name. We can talk about money if you like,
said Hubert, but I can't change her name anymore,
I'm afraid she's stuck with that. Sabrina's a common
enough name. It hardly matters if it's you or a different
one, he said, that's not the point. Sorry, but it just
happens to be the truth. You're young and nice-
looking, but the sculpture is far more about me than
it is about you. I don't want your money, said Sabrina.
Then what do you want? asked Hubert. Sabrina didn't
know what to say, and she ran out of the gallery.

———

She had to trade shifts with someone to get to the
gallery the next morning. At nine o'clock she was
standing outside the locked door. The day was rainy,
and she was glad to find a café from where she could
keep the door in view. The removal men came a little
before ten. Alexandra's eyebrows went up when Sabrina
rapped on the glass door. Hubert isn't here, she said.
I'm not here to see him, said Sabrina, I just want to see
them pack up . . . the sculpture, to say goodbye. Come in
then, said Alexandra, smiling.

It was strange to watch the workmen deal with the
sculpture. They wore thin cotton gloves and picked
her up carefully, and for the first time Sabrina had the
sense that this wasn't her image, but just a piece of
dead metal. The movers wrapped the statue in clear
plastic sheeting and laid her in a padded wooden chest,
fixing her in place with foam rubber mats. They closed
the lid and screwed it down. Sabrina knelt down beside
the chest and put her hand on it. She had the feeling
she was kneeling beside her own coffin. She was again
close to tears, but this time managed to bite them back.

The work wouldn't be collected until the next day,
Alexandra said, showing Sabrina to the door. She told
her about the upcoming show of photographic work by
a promising young woman artist. If you want, I can put
you on the mailing list, and you'll get all the invites.

Sabrina thanked her and shook her head. I'm not really interested in art. Are you sure? asked Alexandra. Do you want me to say hello to Hubert when he next comes in? No need, said Sabrina, and left.

She headed for the city center. It was only eleven o'clock, she had three hours until her shift began. A very fine drizzle was falling, the lakeside promenade was completely deserted. Sabrina felt a great emptiness. Her life, which she had been broadly satisfied with, suddenly seemed insignificant and shallow. She wasn't what mattered, Hubert had said, and that was surely worse than being told that you were ugly or stupid or bad. She now wished he had never spoken to her. Now she was immortalized in her averageness, and she would remain that random girl with a sad expression and a bizarre posture. She sat down on one of the damp benches, pulled up her T-shirt, carefully plucked out her navel piercing and threw it in the lake.

That same day, Sabrina sent Robert Lang an email, and got a reply immediately. His secretary wrote to say Mr. Lang was away on a business trip. We will get in touch with you on his return, she wrote. A week later, she got an email from the collector in person, in the ironic but respectful tone he'd used with her at the opening. He wrote to say that the sculpture was now in his home, he had found a nice place for it, and of course he would be as good as his word, and offered Sabrina visiting rights. Perhaps she could come on Friday at 8 p.m. His secretary would write with the address and instructions how to get there.

Robert Lang lived on the right shore of the lake, the house was one of a group of villas high up on the slope with views of half the lake across to the mountains in the distance. Sabrina had dressed up again, this time she was wearing a short denim skirt and a sheer top. She had had her hair cut short and was wearing dark brown nail varnish. An elderly lady admitted her, greeted her amiably, and told her Mr. Lang was expecting her. She led Sabrina into a large open-plan living room, outside whose enormous windows was a well-kept garden with a pool. Mr. Lang had come to meet them, he shook Sabrina by the hand and asked if she would like a drink. The elderly lady disappeared without a word. You look quite different from the way you looked on the occasion of our first meeting, Robert said, more grown-up, somehow. Have you had your hair cut?

It was strange that the collector seemed less comfortable in his own house than he was in the gallery. After Robert fetched a couple of glasses of wine from the kitchen, handing one to Sabrina and toasting her, there ensued an embarrassing silence. Robert began talking about his visit to Japan, but broke off in midsentence, saying that surely didn't interest her. You're right, she said, and laughed. And you really weren't paid anything for modeling? Sabrina shook her head. I was happy to do it. But that's no reason not to pay someone, said Robert. How much time did it cost you? A day, said Sabrina, a little more than half a day, to be exact. I'd like to give you something for it, said Robert, pulling out his wallet. Sabrina laughed. I'm certainly not taking money from you. What would that look like? No one's watching, he said, laughing as well. No, said Sabrina so firmly that he put his wallet away. Again, there was silence for a while, then Robert said, It's a strange thing for me too, owning this sculpture. If it was molded by hand, or cut out of stone, that would be something else, but it's really as though it was formed directly from your body. There isn't the artist's hand, which is what makes the figure so lifelike. I don't dare touch it. He raised his hands, as though to embrace Sabrina, and let them fall. But you've come to see her. Let's go.

He took Sabrina all over the house, which he evidently lived in alone. The elderly woman seemed to have disappeared. Almost every room contained works of art, sometimes Robert let fall a title or the name of an artist. Most of the items left Sabrina cold, but she didn't let on, and even took trouble to appear interested and ask an occasional question or make a remark.

The sculpture of her was in the library, with her back to the books, looking out over the landscape. That's a good place, said Sabrina, standing next to her image and likewise looking out of the window. From here she has a view of the lake. Do you like water? asked Robert. Yes, said Sabrina, I'm a Cancer sign, crabs like water.

It was night, the lake was only a dark expanse bounded by the lights on the opposite shore, reflected in the water. Sabrina thought about the evening with Robert Lang. They had had a lot of wine to drink and talked about all kinds of things; from the stars they had got on to their families, their hobbies, their relationships, or rather the lack of them, and the fact that they weren't unhappy about it. I never found a woman that made me think she was worth the investment, said Robert. I was always bored by the men who were interested in me, said Sabrina. The idea that they would lay their hands on me and God knows what else gave me hives. I have to touch the patients all day long, that's enough for me. She thought about Jasmin saying the collector was bound to want something from her, but that wasn't it. That's not it, said Robert. I saw it the moment I saw you here—you belong here.

It was warm and quiet, and Sabrina felt pleasantly sleepy. Robert had a cleaner and a cook, he had a gardener who also looked after the pool, a secretary, and a personal assistant. Why shouldn't she join that little select society? Tamara and Jasmin were bound to find her new life boring, but they had never understood what Sabrina wanted from life anyway, and Sabrina had never understood what moved her colleagues. If she was honest, she had never really liked them in the first place.

Sabrina stood by the window of the library and looked out over the lake, she saw the lights on the opposite shore go out one by one and then the long strings of streetlamps. When they came on again in the morning, they were almost invisible because of the fog that lay on the lake. She saw the trains go by, the cars, all the people going to work who would return home in the evening tired and frustrated. She saw the fog thin, and the water of the lake sparkle in the autumn light. Later, it got overcast. Sometimes it rained, or the fog hung around all day. The days got shorter, the trees lost their leaves, the first snow fell. Robert had entered the library, she heard him take down a book and leaf through it. But she knew already that he wasn't there for the book, that he was as impatient and full of expectation as she was. He put the book back on the shelf and came over to stand beside her and look out over the lake. He surveyed the landscape and then her with a gentle, loving look. From the corner of her eye she saw him raise his hand and let it fall. If she could, she would have smiled.

The Woman in the Green Coat

I t was shaming and somehow fascinating how anxiously and fearfully I walked into the hospital, after spending my entire working life there. Ten years ago, I had gone into retirement, and now I was back, but this time I wasn't on the side of the healers, but of those who needed to be healed. At least my way didn't take me through emergency admissions, where I had begun my career; rather, I came in like a hotel guest, with a little suitcase in my hand and a rolled-up newspaper under my arm. The new-look reception even styled itself like the front desk of a hotel, there was a vase of flowers, and glossy magazines in the waiting

area. With a little imagination I could have believed
I was here for a short holiday, not a life-threatening
operation. The specialist had insisted on welcoming
me personally, but since he was just doing his rounds,
the receptionist asked me to wait in the lobby for him.
He'll be along in a minute.

I had just made myself comfortable in one of the
designer armchairs when a woman in a short, lime-
green raincoat entered the reception area. I was a little
surprised by her outfit, it was a balmy day in May and
the forecast predicted more of the same. The woman
had one of those voices that, while not loud, carry; a
voice, furthermore, that seemed familiar, but that I
wasn't able to place. She asked after a doctor whose
name I knew, a gastroenterologist who had joined the
staff just as I was retiring. I couldn't hear what answer
the woman was given.

She was of slim build, and from behind one might
have taken her for a young woman, but when she
turned around and walked into the waiting area, I
saw she was roughly my age. She seemed nervous,
perched on the edge of her chair and fiddling with her
coat. She picked up a copy of a women's magazine,
then straightaway put it back, got up to pour herself a
cardboard cup of water from the water cooler, which
she emptied standing up and dropped in the bin. I

wondered what her trouble was, was she ill herself, or
was she the next of kin to a patient? No sooner had she
sat down again than she leaped up, took a few strides
in the direction of the entrance, and then stopped
indecisively. She seemed to be looking at the vase of
flowers, and now it came to me whom she reminded
me of all along, a patient I had known many years ago,
when I was a junior doctor.

I had just lately taken up my position in the Emergency
Room and was on night shift. It was a Monday or
Tuesday, and things were quiet. I had just gone to get
myself a cup of coffee when the woman on reception
told me a patient had come to see me, but I had time
to finish my coffee, it wasn't anything dramatic. When
I slid aside the curtain to the cubicle, I was a little
startled because a young woman was standing directly
behind it. She was slim and somehow colorless, as
though she'd been less distinctly drawn than the rest
of the world. She was in a dress that looked as though
she had made it herself. She held her right hand away
from her body as though it had little to do with her.
I introduced myself and made to shake hands, then
quickly withdrew once I'd noted my mistake. Miriam,
she said, and held out her left hand. Let me see, I said.

There was a large splinter in the palm, some swelling, and a local inflammation. I asked her how long she had had it. Should I lie down? the woman asked, pointing to the couch at the back of the cubicle. She had a low, warm voice that didn't really go with her skittish, nervous being. No, sit down, I said.

I had to make a small incision to remove the splinter. Miriam watched me without batting an eyelid. I cleaned the wound and stuck a bandage over it. That was it. The woman seemed a little disappointed when I saw her out to the reception area and wished her a nice evening. In the waiting room was a mother and a boy of six or so, who was very pale and whimpering. He fell down the stairs, said the mother as I walked by, it's his foot. I'll be with you in a minute, I said.

The woman in the green mac had spun around on her heel and set off for the West Wing, where the ER was. I left my suitcase and followed her down the narrow corridors that I'd been up and down so many times, but that now seemed so utterly different, a labyrinth I might never find my way out of. The patients, sitting dotted about in little waiting areas, waiting for a consultation or an appointment, seemed to watch me sadistically as I walked by; various terms caught my ear, thigh bone, my daughter, six months. I didn't know how long I would have to stay here, even if the operation was successful. First we'll cut you open, my colleague said, then we'll know more.

The woman seemed to be walking aimlessly along, from one department to the next. Sometimes she stopped, hesitated, went up or down a flight of stairs. She read various notices on corkboards, gazed at the landscape photographs that were displayed on the walls. When doctors came the other way, she slowed her steps as though about to address them, but she never did. One or another of them nodded at her, as though with a vague memory of having treated her at some point. Even though I only saw her from behind the whole time, I grew more and more convinced that it was Miriam, still going around after all those years.

I had the mother and son brought into one of the treatment cubicles and promised to be with them right away. When I stepped outside the building for a smoke, Miriam was still standing there, as though waiting for someone. She asked me for a cigarette. I gave her a light, and we smoked silently and companionably. Miriam blew the smoke out of the side of her mouth and made a mocking expression like someone who had never smoked in her life and has learned the gestures and expressions from somewhere. It was early March, but the last few days had been unseasonably warm. I already had a few night shifts behind me, and as always in those weeks, I was short of sleep, and felt at once incredibly tired and very alert, hypersensitive, and nervous. After a few drags, Miriam gave a whinnying laugh, dropped the cigarette on the ground, and clumsily trod on it. She wished me a nice evening and quickly walked off. I was certain she could sense me watching her, her movements were as self-aware as a model's on a catwalk. She vanished in the darkness, I put out my cigarette and went back to work.

Not many days after this first visit, Miriam was back in the ER. She had come in the afternoon and asked for me, whispered the nurse on reception. When she heard I was still on night shift, she said she would try later.

Miriam asked me if I always worked nights. Tonight's the last time, I said, then I have a week of daytime shifts. Her foot was swollen, she said, she had tripped going down some stairs. This time I let her lie down on the treatment table. She had no socks, only ballet pumps, and her feet were ice-cold. I performed the usual checks, moved her foot this way and that, asked if it hurt and how. Miriam seemed a bit vague, her answers didn't add up and gave no clear sense of an injury. Finally, I had her foot X-rayed. Other patients came in, it was a busy night, and Miriam had to wait a long time till I finally had a moment to look at the X-rays with her and talk her through them. Even though her foot was bothering her, she was pacing up and down in the cubicle when I came back, it seemed impossible for her to sit still. She barely listened to me. It's nothing serious, just a sprain. I bandaged her foot and advised her to wear shoes that would give her more support.

When I came on ward on one of the following mornings, I found Miriam already in the waiting room. She was all alone there, the mornings were usually quiet. She was sunk in thought, then, when I greeted her, she jumped up. I'll be with you right away, I said. The colleague I was taking over from gave me a quick résumé of the night just passed and told me about one or two cases that hadn't been resolved. A young man who had had liposuction a week ago had gotten involved in a fight; he complained of bad stomach pains and refused to be sent home, even though the ultrasound hadn't indicated anything out of the ordinary.

Miriam was already in one of the cubicles, waiting for me. I had only just said hello when I was called away. A worker had been brought in to emergency with a profusely bleeding cut to his arm, and I had to see to him right away. An hour later, I was with Miriam again. She was sitting in her cubicle, smiling, and saying she had stomach pains. Where exactly, I asked her. Here, she said, making circular movements with her hand over her stomach like someone letting a foreign waiter know they were enjoying their dinner. Then you need to see one of my colleagues from internal medicine, I said, I don't know why you've been brought here. I asked for you, she said, you're my doctor. But if you have stomach pains, the other side should be looking after you. Here, we're surgery. Don't you have a GP? Miriam said she didn't think it was that bad. And couldn't I make an exception for her? I asked if she often suffered stomach pains, what she had eaten in the past few days, whether her digestion was normal. On a scale of one to ten, how would you rate these pains? No, said Miriam. She said she had woken up in the night and felt afraid. I gave her a sample package of Panadol and told her to eat regularly and take plenty of liquids. Disappointed, she asked why I didn't want to examine her. She had heard somewhere about ultrasound. I said there was no reason for that. If the pains continue, then you really should see my colleagues in internal medicine. I said she could come to the ER any time, but not for every little trifle. She gave me an offended look, got up and left.

I had expected she would complain to management, but the next day I found a huge bunch of flowers in the day room. They're from your patient of yesterday, said the reception nurse, grinning at me.

The woman in the green mac was still wandering through the corridors, we had been in and out of cardiology and were entering vascular surgery. I was relieved we hadn't run into anyone I knew who would ask me what I was doing. At first I had kept a discreet distance, but the woman hadn't turned around once, and with time I found myself closer and closer to her, without her seeming to notice. She looked briefly into the meditation room as though looking for someone but emerged right away. Once she went into one of the bathrooms, but she didn't stay there long either.

I remembered the time I paid a house call on her and wondered how I'd let that happen. Presumably I'd told myself it was my duty as a doctor to try and help her, but secretly I just liked her, I found her loyalty and trust flattering and that led me to break all the rules of my profession.

That evening, some two or three weeks now after our initial meeting, my phone rang just before midnight. I recognized Miriam's voice right away, she had a slow and pressed way of speaking, as though she had to concentrate very hard not to say something wrong. She said she was in a phone box. She had cut her arm, and could I come. I said she should stick a bandage over the cut. It's quite deep, she said, I've lost a lot of blood. Then ring the emergency number, I said irritably, I'm not on call. Please will you come, said Miriam, and gave me the address. I'm waiting for you.

I picked up my emergency bag and ran down the stairs. I had to wait a long time for the streetcar, and then I had to transfer. Even though it wasn't far, it still took me half an hour to get there. Miriam lived in one of two identical high-rise tenements that were probably built in the fifties and seemed fairly run-down. They stood on the edge of a large park with trees and a playground. Across the street was the football stadium, which, empty, seemed to produce a kind of vacuum, an atmosphere of desolation.

Miriam was wearing a patterned nightdress, and I had to ask myself if she'd really gone out to a phone box dressed like that. Her left forearm was wrapped in a dishcloth that was stained with her blood. Her face was extremely pale. I asked her to sit down and rest her arm on the kitchen table. How did it happen? I asked, carefully unwrapping the dishcloth. There was a cut stretching all the way to the wrist from the center of her forearm, it might easily have severed her pulse artery. Miriam merely watched me with a look of fascination and apprehension. When I examined her arm, I started seeing the many scars on it. Close to the elbow was the clumsy, amateurish tattoo of a small cross in a halo, presumably her own work. I felt a strange attraction, and I couldn't help touching the place on Miriam's arm, very gently. I have no idea how long we sat together like that, joined by my touching her arm. Suddenly I realized what I was doing and pulled my hand away and cleared my throat. It's not as bad as it looks, I said, you were lucky. I'll have to put in a couple of stitches. But at least it's not trivial, said Miriam. I shook my head. No, it's not. I asked whether she owned a car, then I could drive her to the hospital. She shook her head. Couldn't you do it here?

She refused a local anesthetic. She said she had a high pain threshold, and it was true, she didn't so much as flinch as I sewed up the wound. It was as though her arm wasn't part of her. She watched me work, which irked me, I've never known a patient who didn't look away. When I was done, I asked her again what had happened. With a knife, said Miriam. What with a knife? I cut myself with a knife, she said. I bandaged her up and told her to call me tomorrow at the hospital so we could make an appointment to have the stitches removed. She made to get up, but I told her to stay sitting for now. She was still very pale and seemed tired.

I looked around the kitchen, which seemed to be original fifties. On the windowsill were a couple of pots with herbs. The table and chairs were old and looked like junk, but everything seemed clean and tidy. I thought about my own, contemporary kitchen and my apartment, in which I didn't feel at home. About all I made there was coffee, maybe a snack the odd night when I got in late and didn't feel like going out again. It may sound strange, but I felt much more at home in Miriam's kitchen than in my own. I had the feeling I was exactly where I wanted to be.

Then I guess I'd better go, I said, and stood up. I held out my hand, which she took in hers, then brought it to her mouth and kissed it. Wouldn't you stay here? she said.

The woman in the mac had gone down the stairs and into the café. She was now in line for a cup of tea. I stood directly behind her and got an espresso from the machine.

She seated herself at a small table in the middle of the room, while I found a place by the wall from where I could watch her. I hadn't often been in this particular cafeteria. We had a machine on the ward that made better coffee than the equipment here, and I had no great fondness for mingling with the patients. For the first time, I realized how different the patients and the employees were in their bearing, there was no need for hospital gowns and lanyards to tell them apart. You could feel the power the latter had over the former, see it in their confident movements, the certainty with which they sat there talking to one another. So now I was one of the lesser species, the ones who sat there with wide-open, inquiring eyes that looked away when they met mine, as though ashamed of their vulnerability.

Miriam didn't call me to arrange an appointment. Since she had no telephone, I sent her a reminder a couple of days later, was she getting on okay, was the wound healing properly, she should have the stitches taken out, and would we see each other again? I got no reply.

I didn't have many friends, but I was far from being unsociable. I liked debating with colleagues over lunch, talking to the patients and hearing their stories, chatting with the nurses about their holiday plans or trouble with their children or boyfriends. I tended to listen more than speak, there wasn't much to say about me. I was usually one of the last to get up from the table at lunch. Sometimes I would walk an ophthalmologist I liked across to his ward, even though the ER was at the opposite end of the hospital. My colleague asked if I'd already swum in the lake this year. He said he had heard about this neat bathing place, a strip of grass that you sometimes had to yourself. He had heard about it from a patient. She brought me flowers—can you imagine, a huge bouquet. Have you ever got flowers from a patient? What was her name? I asked. You know I'm terrible with names, he said. But from his description there was no other possibility, it had to be Miriam. What was her trouble? I asked. Hard to pin down, he said. A flickering in one eye. I didn't find anything.

That afternoon I rang administration and asked for Miriam's file. The secretary couldn't find the name in the system. At lunch the following day I asked my colleagues about her. There were some who couldn't remember the name, but they remembered the scars on her body, the low voice and the tattoo of the Celtic cross. Miriam had been a patient in at least six wards since the time she first appeared in the ER. Wherever she'd been, she had complained about a vague array of symptoms, pointing to some part and telling some story, visual impairment, headaches, feelings of paralysis, lack of appetite, what have you. Whatever happened to be featured in the advice columns of the women's magazines. My colleague in gynecology had refused to examine her, the others had treated her out of the kindness of their hearts or because they took a shine to her and had then forgotten to ask for her insurance details or issue a bill. It seemed faintly embarrassing to all of them, and I sometimes wondered if they were telling me the whole story. Some had been given flowers by Miriam, they owned up to that, but sooner or later she had stopped turning up for appointments. There's nothing really the matter with her, said the internist, but she's always got something. She's got the lot, said the ophthalmologist, laughing.

My colleagues weren't put out by the way Miriam had unsettled the whole hospital. They talked about other cases, hysterical seizures, false pregnancies, insurance cheats who had successfully faked serious conditions for years, one even blindness. If we didn't have any imaginary patients, we might as well shut up shop, said a dermatologist, whom Miriam had been to see regarding some itch.

The woman in the green mac had stepped out into the park through a rear exit, and I followed her. After a few paces, she stopped to watch an overweight young woman sitting on a bench with a drip stand next to her. She was eating a sandwich and kept tearing off little pieces to feed the sparrows, which were skittering around her feet. For a long time, the woman in the mac stood there watching her, then she spun on her heel and walked past me into the building, apparently without having seen, much less recognized me.

I remembered how Miriam once told me how she liked going to the hospital. She felt safe there. And she liked the park behind the main block, the old oaks and the birches, and the doctors in their white coats. It must be nice to help people, she said. It's strenuous, I said. Often the people themselves don't know what's wrong with them, they can barely tell you what hurts. And what hurts you? she asked. Nothing, I said, but even as I spoke, I knew it wasn't true. If only it were that simple,

I said. In the meantime, I had learned what was wrong, but that didn't make matters any easier.

Miriam had told me about a few of her scars, a burn, a cut, a place on her hip where the skin was red and brittle as parchment. I put my hand on the scars she was talking about, as though by doing that I could make them disappear.

Without my properly becoming aware of it, the woman in the green mac had led me all the way back to the entrance lobby. There stood the chief surgeon. When he saw me, he walked up to me with quick steps, his hand outstretched in greeting. We thought you'd maybe thought better of it, he said laughing and shook my hand. He talked at me, told me about the impending rebuilding of the hospital, the business manager who seemed only to want to cut costs, a lawsuit about a colleague's mistake that had ended well. Only he said nothing about my condition and the upcoming operation, as though it were somehow embarrassing to him that I was now on the other side. He spoke to me as though I was paying a courtesy call, or we had bumped into each other on the street somewhere. Over his shoulder, I watched the woman in the green mac leave the building. For a moment, I thought of going after her, canceling the operation and just leaving and going back to my previous life for as long as it would take me. But then I gave the surgeon my hand, thanked him—for what, I don't know—and walked up to the ward, where they were expecting me.

Cold Reading

Ship always signifies voyage. Don't lose yourself in your desires and dreams. Perhaps it's time to strike out in a new direction.

Although it had looked like rain in the morning, I had left my umbrella onboard ship, and had gone on land with the first group. Barcelona was our fourth stop, after Civitavecchia, Livorno, and Marseilles, and each time I had put myself down for a shore party. I wasn't going to stew on the ship, I wanted to have fun, but the only people who went on the excursions were old couples, people who were interested in palaces and cathedrals and asked well-informed questions and owned expensive cameras that they aimed everywhere, as though they had set themselves to inventory the Pearls of the Mediterranean, as our cruise styled itself.

The odd husband had shot me a look, while their wives were suspicious and quizzed me, and did their best to keep me away from their husbands. As if I had any interest in a flirtation with a retired insurance broker or high school teacher.

A dozen buses were standing ready on the dockside for the trippers. Ours was two-thirds full. The Spanish guide had such a heavy accent that I couldn't understand more than half of what she said, but I wasn't terribly interested in the history of the city to begin with. Our first stop was the Sagrada Familia, the allotted time was just enough to view (and photograph) the cathedral from the outside and to buy postcards and souvenirs, and then it was on into the Barrio Gótico. We inspected the outside of Santa Eulalia, while our guide fed us with useless tidbits of information and my fellow cruise passengers asked clever questions. I had a sudden vision of myself spending the rest of my life in tour groups of elderly persons touring old European city centers and memorizing dates and the names of artists and aristocratic patrons. The tour guide was just saying how thirteen white geese had guarded the cathedral nave, which caused some hilarity in our group. Like little goslings the tourists waddled after the guide who promised to show us arcane corners of the Barrio

Gótico. I watched them go until they had dissolved in the crowd.

In the mornings, the cathedral was closed to tourists. When I walked in, Mass was just being read. I crossed myself and sat in one of the rear pews. I haven't been to a religious service for years, and after a few minutes I knew why. I looked around impatiently, but here too there was nothing but old people. Only the priest was my age, and he was a pretty good-looking fellow. I wondered what he had on under his surplice and whiled away the time imagining myself following him into the vestry and watching as he was transformed from a dignitary to a proper man.

The cruise was Frank's fortieth birthday present for me. He had booked it in spring and was proud of having got it at a steep discount. Too bad that our relationship ended in the summer at the end of six years. A month or so after our final breakup, he gave me a call and suggested doing the cruise after all, but just as good friends, as he said. In fact he had tried to cancel the booking, but the low low price he'd got was not refundable, and as far as his travel insurance was concerned, our breakup wasn't a valid reason for canceling the trip. I said, no chance, I would go by myself, and I'd have a nice time without him. Maybe I'll meet someone, I said, there's meant to be lots of singles on these cruises. I know, it was vindictive of me, but I'd had enough of his miserliness.

The performance at the cathedral started to drag, so I left and wandered on through the old center. Now that no one was telling me what to look out for and which building was built when and for whom, I started noticing much more, the strolling tourists, the workers knocking off in a café for a bit, the scrawny cats, the traders doing their business in the entryways of houses as though they were protecting them from aggressors. Some of the shop windows looked as though they hadn't changed in decades.

The guide had told us where the bus would collect us at the end of the afternoon, but after a short time I'd lost all orientation. It felt like lunchtime, and I started looking for somewhere to eat. None of the restaurants I passed looked likely, and by the time I told myself I'd go into the next one I came to, there just weren't any more. There weren't any businesses in this part of the city either, just seedy-looking tenements, and going from bad to worse, with graffiti on the walls. Then it began raining, to begin with gently. I put up my collar and walked faster, not knowing where I was going. The rain grew stronger, and I ran for a few steps till I came to a covered passage where I could shelter. Wet and out of breath, I stood in the drafty passage and

wondered what I was doing there. I was angry with
Frank, as though the rain was his fault, and with myself
for not having taken my umbrella, and with all the
wretchedness in my life and the world.

The passage led into a yard full of builders' rubble
and all kinds of junk. I wondered if the house and
the back building were even inhabited, that's how
abandoned everything here looked to me. Even though
it was early afternoon, it had gotten chilly and dark, and
I paced back and forth to try and get warm. The rain
by now was sheeting down. I had been standing there
for quite some time when I heard a loud buzzing and
crackling and then a blurred voice, saying in German:
Come on up, second floor, left-hand side. Reflexively,
I pressed down on the door handle, just before the
buzzing stopped. The door slammed heavily behind me.

The stairwell was dimly lit and smelled of damp
and mold. It wasn't until I was climbing the sagging
stairs that I thought it wasn't particularly sensible to
be following the invitation of an unknown voice in a
strange city into an abandoned house. But I was in the
sort of frame of mind where everything was a matter of
indifference to me, and I'd never been timid anyway. In
bad situations I'd managed to defend myself.

The door on the second floor was cracked open,
and a warm light spilled out into the stairwell. I walked

into the apartment. The first thing that struck me was a strong smell of sandalwood and the colored bulbs in the lamps, which gave the room an exotic appearance. Everything here was colorful, the carpet, the furniture, the things on display everywhere. On the hat rack over the coat stand was a stuffed crow, and over the mirror next to it a twinkling chain of colored lights. There were pictures on the walls, old prints of torture scenes and witch burnings, reproductions of icons, a crucifix. I felt I'd stumbled into a curiosity shop or a yard sale.

It wasn't until he began to speak that I noticed the man standing behind one of the doors off the corridor. Won't you take your coat off? he asked in an almost unaccented German, and pressed past me to close the front door. He looked up, as though himself surprised to see such unusual decor, and said, I'm sorry, but there has to be a little fairy dust, people expect it. With that, he helped me out of my coat and hung it up on the coat stand. May I offer you a cup of tea? He led the way into another room, which was just as ornate as the hallway. Here too were colored lamps, thick Persian rugs on the floor, the walls and windows sheeted with patterned material. On a low table of hammered copper stood a wrought iron teapot and a couple of china cups—as though he'd been expecting me. There were nut pastries, of the kind I'd seen in Oriental shops. Kumar, the man introduced himself, and we shook hands. And you're Paula, aren't you?

I wasn't even surprised that he knew my name, that was just one further oddity about this eccentric place. Kumar must have been my age. In the gaudy light it wasn't easy to be sure of the color of his skin, but I rather think he was dark. He was slender, not tall, and his movements were as light and supple as a dancer's. His black hair was short and gleaming, his features were certainly foreign-looking, but I wouldn't have been able to say where he was from, any more than I could place his slight accent. He pointed to a couple of stools and waited for me to sit before sitting down himself and pouring tea. He looked up at me and smiled. He seemed utterly calm, which had the effect of making me nervous. I quickly took a sip of the tea, which was very hot and tasted bitter.

What brings you to me? asked Kumar. The rain, I said, and laughed nervously. Aren't you able to tell me, or don't you know? he asked. Or do you want to test me? That won't be necessary. I don't claim to be infallible. I establish facts, find connections, make prognoses, but what use you make of them is your affair. Whether you classify our meeting as an exotic holiday experience or a life-changing moment doesn't bother me. You mustn't test me, test yourself.

I didn't have a clue what he was talking about.
I only came in because of the rain, I said. And then
I heard your voice over the intercom and came up
here. Your smile must have got you out of a few tricky
situations, no? said Kumar. At least you seem to think
so. That you have the gift of smiling problems away; or
stand over matters and nothing can touch you or rob
you of your composure.

I shrugged my shoulders and was so nervous I took
another sip of the bitter-tasting tea. What's this got in
it? I asked. Kumar hadn't yet touched his. You are an
inquisitive woman, he said, and of course at the same
time you take everything I say for poppycock...No,
no, I don't mind, that doesn't affect me in the slightest.
I mean, I don't believe everything you tell me either.
Maybe together we'll find the real reason for your
coming here. Once the motive has been found, then
the solution isn't far to seek.

Kumar pulled a pack of cards from his pocket and
rapidly shuffled them. Then he laid some out in the
form of a cross and three more in a line on the low
table between us. Past, present, and future, he said. On
the antique-looking cards were figures and symbols and
pictures of people and animals, on one was a heart,
on others, representations of everyday objects, a key, a
whip, but also a fortified tower and a three-master on a

rough sea. While Kumar was setting out the cards, he looked me in the eye and spoke in a low, penetrating voice. You are a discriminating soul. If someone wants to convince you of something, they will need solid arguments. At the same time, you aren't averse to novelty, otherwise you wouldn't be here. You don't leap to judgment. You are a sociable, extroverted person, and it doesn't take a soothsayer to see it. You like to laugh, you laugh a lot. Did you know that women laugh more than men? Less to do with merriment, I suspect, than submission.

I wanted to say something back, and he seemed to sense it, because he raised his palm. No, no, I'm not claiming that you want to submit to me, these are scientific facts, with chance application to individuals. I have the sense that yours is a strong personality. But under the cheerful surface there is a cautious, even reticent woman. You are self-critical, and with a strong desire to be liked and admired by others. There is great potential in you, but you must believe in yourself, allow yourself more space.

I had to laugh. You could say that to pretty much any woman. Who doesn't have a desire to be liked by others? Who's not critical of themselves? This is not about others, it's about you, he said. Suddenly he took my hand. I jumped and wanted to pull it away, but he

held on to it. May I? Don't be afraid, I won't predict
that you will have three children or will suffer a grave
illness or go on a long journey, no cheap predictions.
But I have a better sense of your energy if there is a
physical connection between us. Relax. Leave your
hand be. Trust me, I will hold you.

This was odd. I don't have an esoteric bone in my
body, and was convinced Kumar was a charlatan, a
fraud, but I felt more at ease in his society than I had
for a long time. Perhaps the tea—whatever it was—was
kicking in, my body felt very warm and I felt slightly
tipsy in my head. Everything seemed possible, nothing
mattered. This is the heart line, said Kumar, this is the
destiny line, and the health line. I had finished my tea
and Kumar refilled my cup without letting go of my
hand. He still hadn't drunk any himself.

That tickles, I said laughing, and again tried to free
my hand, but less determinedly. Are you a magician?
A male witch? Forgive me, said Kumar, not letting go.
Here, the Venus mount is lacking definition. Could it
be that your sexual evolution was not unproblematic?
That, when you get to the point, you find it difficult
to let go, and surrender to pleasure? Go on, laugh. You
don't believe that a few lines on your palm are capable
of revealing so much about you? That would fit, you're
not easily persuaded, and that's not a bad thing. You

don't have to believe me. Just ask yourself frankly whether the things I tell you accord with the truth; whether you can recognize yourself in my words.

He looked down at my hand again and traced the lines with his forefinger, but it felt to me less like my palm being read than simply stroked. This line stands for a broken relationship, he said. And at this point, everything becomes blurred. If I'm reading it properly, it says you are currently without a partner. I see a man with whom there was a long relationship, he abused your trust. This experience has shaken you to the core. Can it be that he deceived you? Or you deceived him? I shook my head. At any rate, I see conflicts, said Kumar. A wish for children? I shrugged. You have been seeking, seeking for quite some time now. Perhaps your expectations are too high, you want too much. It's not so much a question of finding the right one as being ready for him. Is it possible that you sometimes get in your own way?

At last he stopped and looked at me, as though expecting an answer to a question. When a woman goes vacationing alone, it doesn't take too much imagination to guess she's single, I said. My tongue felt heavy in my mouth, and I had a job articulating the words. I pulled my hand back, at last Kumar let it go. And if she's a certain age, then there's a pretty good chance she will have been married or in a long-term relationship at least once. As for wanting children, well, you know.

Kumar looked at me in silence for a long time. Then something swung in his face, it looked as though he was dropping a part. He snorted and stood up. It's true, he said, what I said to you about your personality, I could have said to almost all my female clients, and almost all would have recognized themselves in my description. And as far as their problems were concerned, people come to me for the same reasons, you don't need to be a clairvoyant to see that. With young people, it's often an unhappy love affair, with older people it's their health. Middle-aged men usually come because of trouble at work, women have relationship anxieties. It's all just a game, a pastime. But how did you know I was standing in your doorway? I asked. And that you had to address me in German? And how on earth did you know my name? Kumar smiled and raised his hands in perplexity.

He stepped up to one of the windows and drew the curtain. It was little brighter outside, though it was still raining. When I began fortune-telling, I didn't believe in it myself, he said in a soft voice. It was just an easy and convenient way of making a living. Then—he paused, as though looking for the right words—then I began to actually see. I was so overcome by my faculty that I used it pretty mindlessly. I told people the truth about themselves, about their past and their future. Till I realized that that wasn't what they wanted to hear from me. Now I don't tell them anymore what the future will bring, I tell them what they want the future to be. And for that they're grateful, whether it comes to pass or not. I should probably tell you not to be in too much of a rush, that you need to go out of yourself, get involved in something, open yourself to fresh experiences. You will meet the man of your dreams, perhaps you already have, and just don't know it. Do you want to know what will be? What would you do if you could see into the future, if you knew what it would bring? It might be comforting, I said. Or disquieting, he said.

What if he really knew more than other people? The idea was absurd, but also too beguiling to reject out of hand. So you won't tell me anything? I asked, myself getting up and walking over to where he stood. There's nothing to be afraid of, he said. We both looked out the window. I put my hand on his shoulder and had a sense of boundless trust and security. I can see how everything will end, but then it always ends that way anyway. What I can't see is what we make of it, what we'll look back on. And that's what happiness is.

What about the cards? I asked. Hocus-pocus, said
Kumar, and went back to the table. I followed him. He
pointed to the card with the three-master. The ship is
always a journey, he almost gabbled. Don't lose yourself
in your wishes and fantasies. Perhaps you're nearer your
goal than you imagine. The key, he pointed to the card
next to the ship, that will help you find the right path,
and reveal what is deep inside you. And the heart, he
smiled, scooping up the cards and putting them in his
pocket, the heart can be any number of things.

He looked at his watch. Your half hour's up, he
said. I asked him how much I owed him. I had hardly
any money with me and gave him what little I had.
Kumar said nothing, merely looked at me, as though
he was waiting for something. It'll stop raining in a
moment, he said, breaking the silence. At least where
the weather's concerned, it helps to see into the future.
Then you wouldn't have set off without an umbrella.
I could tell it was going to rain, I said, I just didn't
feel like taking it. What was the tea? Did you put
something in it? Lipton's, said Kumar, maybe it was
stewed. He gave me his hand in farewell, but this time
his grip felt less resolute, almost hesitant.

When I stepped out of the building, there was
a young woman who seemed not to know what she

was doing there. I held the door open for her, and said second floor, left-hand side. She seemed not to understand me and shook her head. Perhaps she had just been sheltering from the rain.

Of course it hadn't stopped raining at all, but it was brighter, and the air was as clear as it sometimes is very early in the morning after a chilly night. I felt as though I'd awoken from a dream in which time and space had no meaning. I could hardly believe I'd only been with Kumar for half an hour. He had said many things that had seemed insightful and true to me, had built up a thought structure that seemed harmonious and consistent. But when I tried to remember the pieces, most of it had already slipped my mind, and the rest was as banal as the bits of wisdom on calendar pages or sugar packets. Be yourself, seize the day, the way is the goal, whatever. Still, I felt as content as at the end of a good book or a film I'd enjoyed.

No longer minding the rain, I walked back along the street I'd come on. I was less far from the old town than I'd thought, before long the cathedral loomed up in front of me, and I knew where I was and where I had to get to. I dropped into a restaurant, had a bite to eat, and there were still almost two hours before the bus would take us to the harbor.

When I walked out of the restaurant, the rain had stopped, and the sun had broken through the clouds. So Kumar was right after all, I thought, and had to smile, but then it can't rain forever and ever. Feeling cheerful and optimistic I walked on, full of confidence that Kumar would have been right in everything else he said as well, and that we would see each other again, either in life or else in my memories.

First Snow

Under normal circumstances, the drive to our skiing holiday would not have taken more than three hours, but just behind Zurich the traffic seized up. The children were bickering, Lia said she was bored and Jonas that he was hungry, even though we'd had lunch just an hour ago. It was raining. A black SUV swooped past us and took our place in the lane, causing Franziska to brake sharply and swear. The kids were still being a pain, and Jonas was kicking against my seat. Stop that, I barked at him. Franziska told me not to yell at the children. It's Christmas, she said, pointing to a sign, remember? We could stop and have a coffee.

Great, then we'll never get there, I said, while she already had the turn signal on and was taking the exit ramp to the roadhouse.

Although the lunchtime rush was over, the self-service café was jam-packed, with people pushing and crowding everywhere. American Christmas hits were being played over the speakers, and glittering arrangements of fir-twigs and candles were on the tables and counters. Just as I got to the till, my phone rang. It was Anita. A calamity, she said, sorry, but I need your help. One of our customers, a florist business, was having trouble with the accounting software, and bang in the middle of the Christmas rush. I tried to help them, said Anita, but you know I don't really get those things. Did you try telling them to turn the server off and on? I asked. Anita laughed. Can you give them a call? They're having a meltdown.

The children had found us an empty table and waved us over. I'm just coming, I said, I have to call someone. Was that Anita? asked Franziska, with a little edge of aggression in her voice. Can't they manage without you for a day? I said it was an emergency and it wouldn't take long. Once outside, I lit a cigarette and called the florist's number.

I stood on the terrace among damply gleaming swings and slides, speaking to the manageress,

walking her through the process, and waiting till
she was ready for the next instruction. Through the
plate glass window I could see the children running
around the café, looking like a couple of mime artists.
Franziska was gesturing at me, stony with rage. I
turned my back on her and kicked at a trashcan that
had THANK YOU written on it in four languages. The
manageress read out an error message, and I embarked
on a new set of instructions. When I looked into
the restaurant a while later, there was no sign of my
family. Suddenly the manageress's voice changed.
Now everything's looking like normal again, she said
happily. Then let's hope it stays that way, I said, if not
you can always call me. I gave her my number just in
case and pocketed my phone.

The Christmas hits playing in the restaurant
seemed to have been turned up while I was outside.
Franziska and the kids were nowhere to be seen,
neither in the restaurant nor in the bathrooms on the
lower floor. I asked the cashier, but she just looked
blankly at me and shook her head. I walked out to the
parking lot. The car was gone.

I called Franziska's number and left her a message.
I apologized and said I wouldn't allow myself to be tied
up like that again. Then I went back in the restaurant
and got myself a coffee. The cashier greeted me as

though she'd never seen me before. There weren't any
empty tables, so I moved in with an elderly couple. The
man was scoffing an enormous sandwich, while the
woman was bemoaning her dog's digestive problems.
I stared out the window. A few snowflakes were now
mixed in with the rain, and I was pleased I'd thought to
pack the snow chains. Every couple of minutes I called
Franziska, but she wasn't picking up. Eventually, my
battery went dead and I got up and left.

I had been to this rest stop several times before, but I
only had a dim notion of the surrounding area. It was
like a kind of island where different laws obtained, and
that was completely divorced from the landscape all
around. Set in the perimeter fence I found a little gate,
from where a footpath led into some woods. I followed
the path, first alongside the highway and then across
it through an underpass. I stopped in the underpass,
the ground was littered with trash. I read the graffiti,
obscenities, a few names, a crooked swastika. Someone
had spray-painted a red arrow on the concrete wall. I
followed in the direction it pointed.

The path led along a blocked-up streambed, in
some places great puddles had formed, making progress

difficult. After a bit I left the path and set off into the
woods. The rain had finally given way to snow, which
was now falling quite heavily. To begin with, I'd heard
the roar of traffic on the highway, but it grew quieter,
and finally stopped altogether, as all I could hear was
the sound of my footfall on the snow-covered leaves.
I must have walked for an hour or so in the forest. My
feet were ice-cold and my hair all wet. When I turned
around, I could see my traces feebly marked in a thin
layer of snow. I was glad when I finally hit a track that
led me out of the woods. In front of me was a gently
climbing slope with fields and meadows.

My irritation with Franziska was long since gone,
and I took a quiet delight in the beauty of the snow-
covered hills. In the distance I saw the highway,
with long columns of traffic tailing back in both
directions. The headlights and taillights strung red
and white chains of fairy lights across the landscape.
I thought about the crowds of people when I caught
the train to work in the morning, the queues in the
shops, the hordes of commuters streaming out of their
office blocks at night, into which I merged. And the
Christmas holidays that we wanted to spend in the
mountains as we did each year, it would be no better,
lines at the cable lift station, lines at the ski lifts, lines

in the self-service restaurant. It was my first time alone in a long time, wandering without somewhere to get to, able to go where I pleased.

I walked up the hill. On the horizon an ugly gray two-story building appeared that looked like it might be a factory. Only as I came closer and saw the window decorations did I understand that it was a school. In one window there were lots of paper cutouts that were probably meant to be snowflakes or stars; in another clumsily drawn figures representing the Holy Family, the ox and the donkey and the rest of the cast of the Nativity story. The school stood on the hill all alone, a couple of hundred yards away was a colony of new identikit single-family dwellings that all, apart from their twinkling Christmas lights, looked abandoned.

Snow had come to settle on a car parked in front of the school. I scooped some up into a snowball and let fly at the Holy Family. My first two efforts missed, but the third struck Mary on the head, and the fourth the donkey. A woman appeared in the window, flung it open and shouted: Will you stop doing that right away! Only then did she notice that I wasn't a schoolboy and called: What are you doing there? Can I use the phone here? I called back. She pointed me to the door and disappeared from the window.

The teacher was waiting for me in the doorway. She was younger than I'd taken her to be from a distance, her clothes aged her and the reading glasses she wore on the tip of her nose made her look like the caricature of a teacher. She must have been about my age, with a preternaturally upright carriage, as though she'd swallowed a walking stick. Her face was pretty enough, but the expression on it was severe. She put out her hand before I was anywhere near, and said: Koller. I wiped my snowball-wet hand on my pants and greeted her. Fräulein Koller, she corrected me. I told her the battery on my phone was empty. While she led me through an unlit corridor, she scolded me like a child. What had I thought I was doing, her little second-graders were better brought up than that, and what if I'd smashed a window?

The teacher led the way into a classroom and locked the door behind us. She directed me to one of the little desks. Sit. She took a sheet of paper from a drawer and put it in front of me. I want you to write what prompted you to throw snowballs at the windows. A full side. I looked at her in consternation and said: I'd like to use the phone if I could, Miss. When you've finished, she replied, crossing her arms. I had to laugh. Is that my punishment, then? The rules apply to everyone, she said. She sat down at her desk and went back to her grading.

I don't know what made me obey and start writing. Perhaps I was just too astonished to have been set such a task. Whatever it was, I was happy to be in the warm, my shoes were soaked through, and my toes hurt from the cold. I wrote down what had just gone through my head. That all my life I had moved in long columns of people, that I had always done what was expected of me, had gone to college, married, started a firm, built a house, had children. And that some perfectly inconsequential circumstance had thrown me out of my safe orbit. I wrote that I actually didn't like skiing and hated the crush of other people on the piste, and would much rather have stayed home. Once, Fräulein Koller came over to stand behind me and look over my shoulder. I asked her for a second piece of paper.

I wrote about the snow in my childhood and how I had never been particularly sporty, and the other kids had made fun of me because I couldn't throw snowballs. We had gone sledding but soon lost interest, and the wilder ones among us had started a snowball fight. We formed up into two sides and built fortifications, but when my side went on the attack, I just stayed behind under the snow ramparts, frozen through and breathless with excitement. The noise of

battle gradually grew distant, and it was getting dark,
but I lay there, a lone casualty of the winter campaign
outside the gates of the besieged city. My parents
would weep for me, my name would be chiseled into a
memorial along with those of the countless others who
had lost their lives for the fatherland. It was as though I
could still feel the pathos of my tragic premature death,
the piercing hurt in my hands and feet, when I finally
pulled myself up and ran home. I had never intended to
break the glass, I wrote. I hesitated a moment and then
wrote: I'm sorry.

I stepped up to Fräulein Koller's desk. She kept
me waiting while she got to the end of the paper she
was grading. Then without a word she took the essay
from my hands. As she read, her lips moved, and
she underlined a couple of spelling and punctuation
mistakes, and with her red pen crossed out the clause
in which I said that I'd gone on to have children, then
when she was finished, she nodded and said: Good.
Even if you let your imagination run away with you at
the end a little. She stood up, came around the front
of her desk, and gave me my two sheets back. What's
your name anyway? Georg, I said, and she smiled, and
tousled my hair.

———

When I was standing by the phone in the teachers'
common room, I realized that I didn't know Franziska's
number off by heart. Fräulein Koller had made coffee
and set the tray with the two cups and a plate of
cookies on the large table in the middle of the room.
I've added milk and sugar already, she said. When she
passed me one of the cups, her hand briefly covered
mine. Your hands are still freezing. The coffee was thin
and terribly sweet, and I declined the cookies.

Everyone has their own story, said the teacher, and
stopped, as though considering whether to tell me hers.
Instead, she asked if I at least had a nice Christmas
present for my wife. We haven't given each other anything
for years, I said. That must have been something you
started, she said. She went over to one of the wall closets
that made up an entire wall of the common room and
returned with colored pencils and paper. Why don't you
draw her something? Or would you rather use scissors
and paste? I resisted, but Fräulein Koller wouldn't take no
for an answer. I drew. I was compelled to see that it was
no better than the drawings I'd made when I was a kid. I
drew a bouquet of flowers in a vase. Fräulein Koller cast a
critical eye on me throughout. When I was done, she said
I ought to write a nice message on it: For Mama, Happy
Christmas. She's not my mother, she's my wife, I said, and
wrote: Dear Franziska, Happy Christmas at the foot of

the drawing. I asked Fräulein Koller if there was a bus stop
anywhere near, or a railway station. She shook her head.
The buses only go during school hours. The last one went
hours ago.

Fräulein Koller drove an ancient Ford Fiesta. Instead
of an antenna, it had a piece of wire clothes hanger
attached to the roof, and the passenger side door could
only be opened from the inside. I tried to belt myself
in, but the thing jammed. Fräulein Koller leaned across
me and jerked at it until it yielded. Her body brushed
mine, and for the first time I had a sense of her as a
woman and imagined taking her in my arms. On my
lap was the drawing of the vase of flowers that I'd done
for Franziska. The windowpanes were misted over.
Fräulein Koller turned on the ignition and moved the
air temperature to maximum. Classical music could be
faintly heard under the roar of the heater. Do you like
Brahms? she asked.

We drove down little country roads, I had no idea
where we were. Then the teacher dropped me off at
a tiny station I'd never heard of. I wanted to give her
some money to thank her, but she shook her head.
You can't buy everything with money, she said in her
teacherly way, and we shook hands.

———

The train came in half an hour. I looked out of the window and watched dark silhouettes glide by, with the occasional lit-up window. I imagined Fräulein Koller sitting at home by now. She was in the kitchen of her small apartment, making supper for herself, something healthy with fresh herbs and just a pinch of salt. She carried her supper into her living room, which was decorated with photographs of her parents, of nieces and nephews, maybe a reproduction from a calendar, something from Chagall or Kandinsky. And then I thought about our house, which right now was empty, and in my mind I walked through the unlit rooms and tried to pick up clues about the people who lived in them, and who, quite suddenly, felt as alien to me as that solitary woman teacher.

I had to change trains twice, each time with my ridiculous drawing in my hand. I must say, I did think about throwing it away. By the time I got to Tiefencastel, the last postbus was long gone. In a phone booth by the station I found the number of a taxi firm. The driver said he had another customer, but he'd pick me up in half an hour. There wasn't a restaurant anywhere near, so I walked up and down freezing in front of the station building, till the taxi finally arrived

forty minutes later. It was past eleven by the time we
reached the chalet. All the windows were lit up, and
when I climbed up the outside stairs, Franziska opened
the door. She flung her arms around me, as though we
hadn't seen each other for weeks. You're all covered
in scratches, she said, and helped me out of my coat.
That must have been when I was in the woods, I said,
and handed her my drawing. You can't imagine what
happened to me.

On our way back from the skiing holiday, we stopped
off at the rest stop again. After we'd had something
to drink, I said to Franziska and the children, I want
to show you something. I took the next exit and
went back. I couldn't orient myself and ended up
crisscrossing the whole region. I'd forgotten the name
of the station where Fräulein Koller had dropped me
off, and however hard I tried, I couldn't find either
the station or the school building again. The children
went to sleep. Franziska said maybe I had just imagined
everything.

I went back onto the highway. It was getting dark,
and the evening rush hour was under way. The cars
tailed back, and at the top of one valley, I again saw
the chain of red taillights, but this time they had a

strange beauty for me, they were an emblem of what connected me to the rest of mankind, who were all, like me and my family, on their way home.

The drawing I had made for Franziska was still hanging on our fridge years later. Whenever our friends asked about it and said dumb things about it when they learned that it was mine and not one of the kids', each time Franziska would say: That was the best Christmas present I ever had from Georg.

Dietrich's Knee

Adrian had gone up into the room in the afternoon, even though Sabine wouldn't arrive before six. He turned up the thermostat, drew the curtains, and folded back a corner of the sheet. Then he sat down in a chair by the window and contemplated the empty bed. He couldn't help picturing to himself Sabine and Dietrich doing all those things they'd written to each other about in the past nights. They were standing by the window, gazing down on the street, at the passersby on their way home, or God knows where. Dietrich was standing just behind Sabine, and he was kissing her neck very softly, she was tipping her head to the side, then Adrian imagined her closing her eyes and smiling. She was breathing noisily. Dietrich was gripping her by the waist, and then she turned around and they started to kiss, first quick, brief kisses, then long and passionate.

They were lying in bed together naked, Sabine on her front, and Dietrich was stroking her back, running his finger down her spine. Sabine turned around and looked at Dietrich. Is it really you? she said and smiled in astonishment. Come! Adrian couldn't bear it any longer, he jumped up out of the chair and ran down to the hotel bar to wait for her.

He was the only customer, the bar seemed only just to have opened. He sat down at a corner table and waited impatiently for the waiter to come and he could order a beer. Sorry, he called out, after the waiter had already turned, make that just an espresso and a glass of water.

He had never been here before, why should he, after all he lived in the city and had no cause to take a hotel room. He imagined Sabine sitting here with Dietrich, exchanging glances, their knees touching under the table. I thought it was the table leg, Sabine had written in her first email. Maybe she really had. Three weeks ago they had met at a conference for advertising campaign managers, and a week later Dietrich had sent her the first email.

The waiter was busy behind the bar. From time
to time he raised his head and looked over at Adrian.
He switched on the stereo, and music poured from the
loudspeakers. Briefly, Adrian had the sensation that
it was night and the bar was crowded with people,
dancing and having a time. The waiter turned the
volume back down, changed the CD, and smooth jazz
came out. Adrian tried to identify the title, it was the
instrumental version of a song he knew. Only when
he started humming along did the words spring to his
mind: *They're writing songs of love, but not for me . . .*

If Adrian had still been working, none of it would
have happened. Last year, the agency had lost two
important clients, and after a couple of months in
which he'd tried to keep himself busy, Johannes had
called him into his office and told him he'd have to
let him go. There was a second writer in the agency,
but he was a partner, and hence untouchable. Sabine
had her salary, said Johannes, and he would try to put
occasional freelance jobs his way. Don't be angry with
me, he'd called after Adrian, who'd furiously charged
out of his office.

Adrian poured more water into his glass. He noticed
his hand shaking as he thought of his sacking. That
evening Sabine had said he should try and understand
where Johannes was coming from. If there was no work,

there was nothing he could do about it. You knew in advance, didn't you? said Adrian. She sat down, looked down at the table, and then looked him straight in the eye. Of course I knew. I'm on the board. When did you make the decision? How long have you known? What does it matter, said Sabine, it was Johannes's job to inform you. It has nothing to do with you personally. And after all, you'll profit if the firm does well. He should make an effort to see things positively. He had time now to write the novel he'd been talking about forever. And by the time he was off benefits, everything would look completely different. All that social guff the whole time, said Adrian, but when it's money that's involved, you're all just as brutal as anyone else.

The loudspeakers were now putting out "I Got Rhythm," that was an easy pick. *I got rhythm, I got music, who could ask for anything more . . .* A job wouldn't hurt, thought Adrian. The first couple of weeks, he actually had tried to get going on his novel, but he'd been crippled. He kept starting over, pushed the characters around in his mind and diagrammed the plot and timelines on large sheets of graph paper. He even bought a guide, *How to Write a Bestseller*, but none of it helped. One evening he told Sabine the story. She looked at him sardonically and told him it was something Philip Roth had written half a century ago.

The next day, Adrian tossed his drafts and notes into the trash. Then he went to the gym and ran on the treadmill until he was done.

Early on, Sabine would tell him every evening what had happened that day in the agency, and who had done what and said what to whom. But in the course of time she dried up. Everything was just as usual, she said, and when she asked, it was he who didn't tell her what he'd done with his day. Oh, nothing, he said. It was true. Once or twice he had got jobs from the agency, little PR texts for a lamp designer he'd done work for previously. Other than that he had nothing to do and did it. Was it asking too much if he helped out in the home a bit? said Sabine, when she got home and found the breakfast things in the sink. You threw me out, said Adrian, it's not my fault I'm out of a job. Sabine shrugged her shoulders, and the dishes went clattering into the dishwasher.

Increasingly, Adrian had the feeling she was bored with him. She seemed dissatisfied and gave irritable replies to harmless questions. Sometimes he caught her frowning at him. But when he asked what the matter was, she said nothing, and went on leafing through papers she'd brought home from work. If they'd quarreled, at least then there might have been a reconciliation.

———

One morning, Sabine forgot her laptop at home. She had overslept and went running out of the apartment without breakfast. An hour later, she phoned. Adrian still hadn't got dressed, he was sitting in the kitchen, drinking coffee and flicking through the supermarket leaflets that came with the paper. Sabine asked him to email her a document she'd been working on the night before. She gave him her password, and he told her she needed a better one. Then she guided him through the folder till he'd found the file she wanted.

She said thank you, and sounded kindlier than she had in a long time, almost chirpy. She asked him what he was planning to do. She had a meeting coming up, but thought she'd dash home during her lunch break, she was unable to work properly without her laptop. If Adrian felt like it, they could eat some lunch together. Will you cook us something? Before she hung up, she told him he wasn't to snoop. She said it lightly, almost jokingly, but suddenly Adrian asked himself whether she was hiding something from him.

The computer had sent the document and received three new emails. Almost automatically, Adrian read the subject lines. One was an advertisement for men's socks, one was from Sabine's friend Isabelle, with whom she occasionally went to the cinema or the theater. The third said: Dietrich's Knee. Adrian knew no one called Dietrich. He hesitated, then opened the email. It was just a few lines.

Dear Sabine's Knee,

We were getting along so well under the table, then suddenly you were gone. Apparently, your Sabine had a headache. Once you were gone, my Dietrich took me upstairs right away. I think he might have been missing your Sabine. Anyway, he raided the minibar, which he never normally does, being far too mean. I'm wondering: will we see each other again sometime? My Dietrich is going to be in Karlsruhe (he'll be there from 3–5 May, but he's tied up in the daytime). But perhaps you'll have time for a beer or whatever there is for knees to do there in the evening? By all means, bring your Sabine. She can have sensible conversations meanwhile with my Dietrich. He says hello, and so do I.

Dietrich's Knee

Adrian stopped. Sabine had told him about some Dietrich when she came back from her conference last week. An ad executive from an agency in Stuttgart, if he remembered correctly. She had told him something he had said, but Adrian couldn't remember what it was, only that Sabine had found it incredibly funny. So there was more, an advance, which Sabine seemed to have repulsed.

He was about to turn the computer off when he remembered that the server would show the message as having been "read," which would betray him. On the other hand, if he deleted it, this Dietrich was sure to write again. He didn't sound like someone who was easily put off. And his next email would reach Sabine. Nothing seemed to have transpired between the two of them, but the way Sabine had been behaving of late, he wouldn't put it past her. If he wanted to find out if she was loyal to him, he had to find a way of getting the story to go on.

Adrian prowled around the apartment, thinking. In the end, he opened a couple of new accounts from a free email service, calling one of them Dietrich's Knee, and he was going to call the other Sabine, but that name was already taken, and the program offered him Sabine867. Sabine's laptop had entered powersave, and Adrian was pleased now that her password was so straightforward. He copied Dietrich's email and re-sent it to Sabine from the new address. He deleted the original.

He and Sabine ate lunch together. He felt guilty, but he was also wondering whether and how she was going to reply to Dietrich. She was still in a good mood and was talking about a big client she was going to be presenting to in a couple of weeks. She said she thought she'd probably be doing some overtime in the near future. Adrian said he had plenty of spare capacity. If we land the contract, you'll be back on board, said Sabine.

After the late news, Adrian left the TV running. He watched a talk show on euthanasia. Sabine had her laptop on her knees and was typing. Are you working on your presentation? he asked. She nodded and said Isabelle wanted to see a film with her next week. Was that okay with him? You're a free agent, said Adrian. You and I could do something too, you know, said Sabine vaguely, and started typing again. Adrian looked at her. She must have read Dietrich's email, perhaps she was even now replying to it. He turned off the TV and said he was going to bed. Sabine said she'd be along in a minute. When he brushed a kiss on her lips, she turned the screen away as if to hide something from him. Is your project so hush-hush, then? he asked. It's about launching an alcohol-free beer, said Sabine. If you have any ideas . . . I only work for money, said Adrian.

He was still awake half an hour later when Sabine slipped into bed beside him. She seemed restless and he couldn't help wondering if she wasn't thinking about that Dietrich person. After a while she got up and crept out of the bedroom. The luminous hands on the alarm showed twelve-thirty. By the time she came back to bed, Adrian was asleep.

The moment Sabine was out of the house the next day, he checked the email. Sabine had replied to Dietrich; the email went off last night at a quarter to one.

Dear Dietrich,

I didn't notice a knee that evening. I must have taken it for a table leg. I suppose I really ought to tell you off for your boldness. You know very well I'm in a steady relationship, and if I rightly remember, so are you, knees and all. What are you going to be in Karlsruhe for?

Best wishes, Sabine

Adrian was mollified. Except the sentence about really ought to tell you off. So why didn't she? For a moment he was tempted to alter the sentence, but in the end he copied the email, just adding a PS, that he was to use this address, because mail at her other one

could be read by anyone in the firm. He forwarded
the message. When he checked the new accounts at
lunchtime, he saw there was already a reply.

Dear Sabine,

even being told off by you is a pleasure. I was
worried you wouldn't remember me. I only hope
the leg you felt was not the table leg, because then
I might have been playing footsy with your boss.
(And I think he likes you better than he likes me.)
I'm going to Karlsruhe to make a rival presentation.
Alcohol-free beer, wouldn't you know it. Not my
favorite, but the budget is eye-popping, and we have
a few decent ideas.

Two pecks on the cheek and one on the knee,

Dietrich

Sabine's reply was not long in coming, presumably
she was on break and sorting through her personal
correspondence.

Dear Dietrich,

then I'm afraid we are indeed rivals because
my firm is also pitching for the budget you so aptly
describe. In which case it'll be more a case of elbows

*than knees for us. I hope you do well, and that we
beat you.*

Best wishes, Sabine

That afternoon, three more emails pinged back and
forth, all faithfully forwarded by Adrian. Dietrich was
on offense, Sabine fended him off. But the speed of her
replies made Adrian suspicious. She repelled Dietrich's
advances, wrote that she was a good girl, which to
Adrian sounded a little laughable, but she seemed to
be getting a kick out of the game anyway. Adrian went
into the kitchen to make himself some tea. By the time
he was back, Dietrich had already replied:

Dear Sabine,

   *I too am, at bottom, a good boy. Perhaps it's
best if we don't see each other and don't fall into
temptation to spy on one another or worse. I will
desire you from a distance. And I'm sure we'll see
each other sometime.*

   Good luck with your pitch.

Sincerely, Dietrich

A good boy? thought Adrian, you're a wet rag,
giving up at the first sign of resistance. If you're serious
about conquering Sabine, you have to make some

effort. This time, he adapted Dietrich's message before forwarding it.

Dear Sabine,

I too am, at bottom, a good boy. Maybe with the usual professional deformation—too much imagination, or maybe curiosity. Sometimes that crosses the virtue. But then I refuse to believe you're quite as good as you say you are. Or am I mistaken about that? Being rivals surely shouldn't keep us from meeting over a drink in Karlsruhe. Maybe not alcohol-free beer, but a glass of wine instead? What about it?

Dietrich

Sabine must have written her reply on the way home, because it was practically simultaneous with her text to Adrian, telling him she was running slightly late.

Dear Dietrich,

I see, so I look like a good girl, do I? Or are you just trying to provoke me? Email is certainly not the place to do it. Meeting a man in a bar is still permissible; two knees under a table likewise. The red line, I would say, is between the bar and the hotel room. Where will you be staying, in Karlsruhe?

Yours, Sabine

Adrian remembered how he and Sabine had first got together; it was not dissimilar. They had been colleagues for a while, and had traveled together to a presentation in Frankfurt. The evening after the presentation, they had celebrated, even though they didn't yet know if they had landed the contract. The agency was generous with its per diems, and they had gone to the most expensive restaurant they could find. Adrian had always thought it was he who had seduced Sabine, but when he thought through the evening in detail, he realized it was she who had taken the first steps. Over dinner, she had laughed a lot, often for little reason, and had gazed into his eyes for long periods, without saying anything, but with a suggestive smile. On the way back to the hotel, she had linked arms, under the pretext of being a little inebriated. Then in the hotel, she had suggested a nightcap, as she put it. The hotel bar was just closing, but in the elevator, Sabine said there was always the minibar.

Dear Sabine,

> *surely sometimes a smile or a long stare in another's eyes can cross the boundaries of what's permissible. Or if the bar where two people meet*

*happens to be a minibar. I wouldn't mind going with
you as far as that frontier. And if there why not
beyond?*

Your Dietrich

Sabine had helped herself to a miniature of
whiskey, Adrian had taken a beer. He had turned out
the main light and they had gone over to the window
and looked out. Suddenly Sabine had spun around and
kissed him on the lips.

Back in the agency, they had remained discreet
about the fact that they were a couple. It was after
it got out that the problems with Johannes began.
First he had promoted Sabine to the board, even
though Adrian had been there longer, and then he
had effectively sacked him. Of course, none of it had
anything to do with the fact that Johannes might have
had the hots for Sabine. Humiliating a rival was just a
pleasant side effect.

Dear Dietrich,

*I haven't crossed any boundaries for a long time,
and I'm a bit leery of doing so. But I will admit that
the idea is not without its appeal. A meeting at a
minibar would have the advantage of discretion. We*

are after all competitors—perhaps it's best that we
not be seen together. How do you picture our meeting
thereafter? Would knees be involved?

> *A little breathlessly,*
> *Sabine*

When Adrian had merely been forwarding Dietrich's
emails, he had been a little envious of their flirtation;
now that he was writing to Sabine himself, he had the
feeling she was flirting with him, even if she thought he
was someone else. He thought back to that first night
in the hotel, and wished they could be like that again,
without all the domestic clutter, the dirty dishes, the
piles of laundry lying around, their bickering and moods.

Dear Sabine,
I'm picturing a darkened room.
*   You've got a whiskey from the minibar, I've got*
a beer. We are standing by the window, I am just
behind you. I hold you by the waist, then you spin
around and we kiss.

> *Your Dietrich*

Just after Adrian had sent off this last, he heard
the door go. He went out into the hall to welcome
Sabine home. She was reading something on her

mobile, but the instant she saw him, she stuffed it in her bag. How was your day? she asked, letting him kiss her. He hadn't gotten around to the shopping, but Sabine was calm, and said there was probably the rest of some goulash she'd made last month. They ate it, without talking much. When Adrian looked up from his plate, he thought he saw Sabine looking at him, but she quickly looked away and got up to clear the table.

They moved to the sitting room. He sat on the sofa, Sabine in a chair, both with their laptops out. Are you working on something? asked Sabine. Just reading the paper, he said. And answering a couple of emails. What about you? I need to go over the concept for the brewery and put in the finishing touches, she said. It's up for discussion tomorrow. She typed away while Adrian played patience. When he looked over to her, he thought she was blushing faintly. She smiled, looking younger than her years. He wished he could have crossed the room and kissed her.

Dear Dietrich,

You're a bold one. Just a moment ago, we were having a drink together, and now we're kissing. Are you always in such a hurry with your conquests?

Sabine

*I was just picturing you sitting at home and smiling
as you're writing to me,*

Dietrich

*How do you know I'm home? I could be sitting in
my office working on the rival presentation that will
knock spots off yours.*

S.

*I don't think so. You never told me what you thought
of my fantasy. I wonder if I'm in for a kiss or a slap.*

D.

A slap followed by a kiss.

S.

Adrian was simultaneously excited and indignant.
He looked over at Sabine, who was typing something,
hesitating, then pressed a button with an expression
on her face as though she were detonating a bomb,
whereupon she closed her laptop. Adrian was about to do
the same, when You Have Email appeared in his in-tray.

*PS. Incidentally, I have just broken up with
my boyfriend, and am prepared for all kinds of
naughtiness.*

Adrian gasped. Even though he had been
wondering for a while now how much longer Sabine
would stick it out with him in his recent frame of
mind. To learn of it so suddenly was still a shock. Not
least the fact that he didn't hear it from the horse's
mouth but rather that she was writing it to a man she
barely knew, as though it had been something of no
importance.

I am a married man!!

He typed this and sent it off, but Sabine was
already gone, she probably wouldn't get to see it
tonight. When he walked into the bedroom the lights
were already out, but no sooner had he slipped under
the covers than she scooted over to him and started
kissing him with a passion he no longer associated with
her. While they made love, he wondered if it was for
the last time, whether Sabine meant to kick him out
afterward. Are you crying? she asked, laughing, and
passed her hand across his face. What's the matter?

He slept badly that night. He asked himself when
and how Sabine meant to break it to him. Two years
ago he had moved in with her and given up his own
apartment. She would throw him out—and he couldn't
even blame her. He paid his share of the rent, but she

would have no trouble taking care of it herself. His unemployment money on the other hand would never stretch to a nice apartment, at the most a furnished room somewhere. And he could be sure he wouldn't be given any more work by the agency, Sabine certainly wouldn't want to have any contact with him after their split. He saw his whole life going down the tubes, and all because of some idiotic type from Stuttgart.

At breakfast, Sabine was in a glorious mood. She talked about the campaign they had planned, *100% beer, 0% alcohol*. She asked him for his opinion, but he didn't know what to say, his thoughts were going around in a whirl, he could think of nothing but their separation and its consequences for him. No sooner had Sabine gone than he switched on the computer and started looking for jobs and a room in the appropriate places, he wanted at least not to be caught wholly unprepared.

No one seemed to need a creative, only when he broadened out his search did he find a couple of job offers. An insurance firm was looking for a press agent, and there were a couple of posts for substitute teachers—his original job. He drew up a CV, found his various reports and degrees, and made a bunch of scans. It was still before noon, and he was on his way to the letterbox to post four applications. The quest for

a room or studio apartment was harder. But perhaps
Sabine wouldn't object if he stayed for a while in the
guest bedroom, they hadn't had a falling out, it was just
that Sabine had had enough of him.

He spent the afternoon clearing up his things,
washing clothes, and tidying the apartment. He bought
groceries, and hesitated at the flower stand. He hadn't
bought Sabine flowers for a long time; it would be
a little disingenuous to do so now. But then he had
nothing to lose, and he bought a bunch of tulips.

It was only after putting the groceries away in
the fridge and setting the flowers in a vase that he
remembered to check on the emails. Sabine had
written back that morning, on her way into work,
tersely:

Cold feet, my champion?

He wondered what to write in reply. Ideally,
nothing at all, but then the whole cheat would be
exposed, and Sabine would throw him out right away.
Should he make it appear that Dietrich had indeed got
cold feet? But on the basis of the emails he'd already
written, that was unlikely. Anyway, he had to assume
that Sabine would take it up with Dietrich when they
met. Finally, Adrian decided he would try and drive

the matter to a resolution. He would see how far Sabine was prepared to go. If she agreed to meet Dietrich in a hotel room, he would at least have had a moral victory.

Dear Sabine,

the temperature of my feet is in line with statistical averages. But I didn't want to impose on you. If you have time next Tuesday, I would be happy to welcome you to my minibar.

Your Dieter

Half an hour later came Sabine's reply.

No fantasies today? No double entendres? No kisses for my knees? Tuesday evening should be okay, the earlier the better. I won't be able to stay long, but a lot of things can happen in a couple of hours.

S.

After more emailing back and forth, they agreed on six o'clock. Send me a text with your room number, wrote Sabine, and once again Adrian was surprised at the degree of boldness and forward planning with which she was prepared to deceive him.

When Sabine came home, Adrian had already made supper and laid the table. What's all this? she asked. Have you got something you mean to tell me? Or is this a proposal? She laughed readily, as though she'd said something terribly witty. I just felt like cooking again, said Adrian. And doing the laundry and cleaning the apartment? asked Sabine, with raised eyebrows.

All day Adrian had asked himself when Sabine was going to tell him. Would she wait until the weekend so that they'd have time to talk? Or would she have her meeting with Dietrich first, and present him with a fait accompli? I'm sorry, there's someone else. But what would she do when she realized that the Dietrich who had made the improper suggestion to her didn't actually exist? Certainly not go back to her old boyfriend with her heart full of remorse—that wasn't her style at all. Still less if she noticed that he'd lured her into a trap.

After supper they sat as they had the day before, with their laptops out in the living room. Adrian again claimed to be reading the paper and Sabine that she was working. No sooner had she settled herself than there was the first email to Dietrich. Sabine wanted to hear about the fantasies he owed her. Or was he intending just to pootle off home after their kiss by the window? Adrian wrote her one email in which he asked how her boyfriend had taken their parting, if everything was

all right, but then he didn't send it, for fear of arousing
Sabine's suspicions. Instead, he let his imagination run
a little more, wrote about undressing her and embracing
her and making love to her, he couldn't help noticing
how leaden it all sounded. Sabine wrote away on her
laptop, but no reply arrived. Perhaps she was working
on the presentation after all. Adrian was about to send
a second email, apologizing for the poverty of the first,
when her answer came. She wrote to say that she liked
his ideas, but did they really have to make love on the
floor, when there was a bed nearby? Then she described
her sense of their encounter, and from that point on,
the emails came and went in an accelerated tempo. The
irony of the first messages was replaced by a directness
that surprised Adrian in himself as much as in Sabine.
They made love in words, and perhaps it was the lack of
resistance from any reality that led them to go further
than they might have done in an actual encounter.
Sometimes Adrian sneaked a look at Sabine. He had
the sense that she wasn't really present, it was as though
her soul had left her body and was moving through the
fictive spaces of her imagination.

All weekend Adrian was nervous. He felt like a prisoner,
waiting for his sentence to be handed down. Sometimes

he thought Sabine had changed her mind. But buying her flowers and cleaning the apartment was never going to do that. On Sunday afternoon he was on the point of raising the matter himself, just to get some certainty. At supper, Sabine said she and Isabelle were planning on going to the cinema on Tuesday. He didn't even ask what the film was, he wouldn't have been able to stand hearing her lie further. She might get home late, she said, Isabelle had said there was something she wanted to talk to her about. Boyfriend trouble, I suspect.

"Stormy Weather" came over the loudspeaker, and Adrian identified it right away. He looked at his watch for about the hundredth time since he'd been there, it was just before six. He had booked the room under the name of his rival, but once he'd gone up there, and was about to text Sabine the room number, he realized that of course his phone would give him away. So he had decided to wait for her down in the bar, which had a view of the hotel lobby. Maybe he was secretly hoping that she wouldn't come if he didn't write again, that she would get the cold feet she had taunted Dietrich with having.

Suddenly there was Sabine in the hall. Adrian's heart bounced just as it did early on in their relationship, when he was so excited before each meeting that he couldn't even eat. She was wearing the little black dress he so liked, dark stockings, and the only pair of heels she owned. If he hadn't known her for such a long time already, he thought he might easily have fallen in love with her there and then.

Sabine stood in the hall cluelessly for a moment, looking around. Then their eyes met, but she seemed not to be alarmed, she smiled and walked toward him with uncertain steps. Dietrich? she inquired, still smiling, and sat down opposite him. Adrian nodded. I'm a bit excited, said Sabine and laughed nervously, I don't do this kind of thing every day. Nor do I either, said Adrian, and it was all he was capable of saying.

It's Getting Dark

What I remember? That everything was still the way it was then. That it was colder inside than out and that it was dark. After hours outside it took me a long time to adjust to the lack of light. The hearth with the open fireplace, the rough-hewn table, the benches, the basin, all of it old and worn. Still no electricity or running water. Ladles and pots hanging on nails in the walls, a small hatchet, an almost blind mirror that made my face look so creased, it was as though I'd aged by decades overnight. There were barely any provisions, dried spaghetti, a couple of tins, instant coffee. Standing out like will-o'-the-wisps, the various plastic items: a pink bowl, a blue jar of hand cream, a red tube of toothpaste, three toothbrushes in different shades, two of them for children. Also the light green rubber boots by the door in child sizes, and the shrill yellow waterproofs hanging above them.

A door to the left led into the little cubbyhole, the mattress room, where I and my brother had slept. A tiny, begrimed window gummy with spiders' webs. A nest of sleeping bags and quilts, crocheted blankets, and pillows in plaid cases. Two worn stuffed animals pressed into a corner, as though in terror. A pervasive smell of dust and dirty hair.

On the opposite side, the little room where our mother had slept, with table, bed, woodstove. On a rough plank shelf, books about regional plants and animals, maps and board games, feathers, a couple of curious-looking rocks, or perhaps they were bones? On the walls, clumsy drawings of the mountains, ponds, the hut itself, a reflection of the world that surrounded us. Sheep and cattle, chamois goats, marmots, scribbled birds, a girl and a boy, maybe. The drawings were signed. Luca and Annina.

It was in the inn that I first got to hear about the woman and children. No one had actually clapped eyes on her, they had only heard it said by X or Y that they had been seen in the distance, or encountered on the Schattgaden, near the Langwand, that smoke had been seen coming out of the chimney on the Silberenalp at nightfall, even though the herders had driven their cows back down into the valley weeks ago now.

Who was it who saw them? I asked. Who ran into them? No one was sure. Hunters, hikers, the man called Anton Betschart? But when I called him, he didn't know anything. But he too had heard tell of the woman and her children, he couldn't remember from whom. The next day, I called my boss in Schwyz to ask what I should do, and if I should walk up to the hut? He demurred. Hunters talked a lot, given the chance. Maybe the schnapps had gone to their heads, either that or the fog. When I passed the inn at midnight, I saw there were still lights on. Half a dozen men were sitting there, and the mysterious woman and her children were still the subject. Maybe they were refugees hiding out up there, said someone, what if they starved or froze to death, then there'd be the usual reaction. A woman running away from her husband and taking the children with her, maybe from the Glarnerland. Then there were the old stories of people who had vanished up there and were never seen again, stories that were at best half-true. The men—all bar one—looked at me, and he said the police ought to go up and have a look. No one would have told me to my face. I told them all to go home. I don't want to see anyone here in fifteen minutes. They grumbled quietly, they didn't like being bossed around by a woman, not even—or maybe especially not—by a woman in uniform.

I'd broken up with my boyfriend that spring. The reasons don't belong here. We had met at the police academy and had gone on being thrown together so much on the job that when we broke up, I'd gotten myself transferred up here, a long way away from him, to the valley where I'd spent the first ten years of my life. Unfortunately, the village had changed while I'd been away—or maybe I'd changed—anyway, I felt less at home up here than in the city where I'd been living until recently.

The next free day I had I decided I'd go have a look-see up on the Silberenalp. I packed some provisions and drove up to the pass. The trek through the karst was hard, but I love the wildness and remoteness of the area, regardless of what has happened here. The landscape isn't to blame, it has no memory, no past, it's always just what it is in the moment, what it always has been. The pale gray weathered rock seems alive, water has carved it into organic forms, washed runnels in the limestone, forming holes and fissures in which ferns, grasses, and Alpine roses have taken root. The past lies under the karst in the form of a gigantic system of caverns formed over millions of years, of which only the least part has so far been explored.

On the high plateau several six-foot cairns stood like silent guardians. From the highest of them rose a rusty metal cross, as though it was a matter of putting up some deity to oppose the mountain spirits. In a cleft in the stone pyramid was a blackened can containing a summit book, a plain spiral notebook and a ballpoint pen. Some hikers had entered only their names and the date, others specified the route they had taken, and a few had added some remark about the beauty of the scenery, the awful weather, a pair of lovers had drawn a heart beside their names. The most recent entry was undated, just a single name, Thomas. I wrote my name there, put the notebook back in its place, and hiked on.

After another couple of hours or so, I saw the alp at my feet. As I descended, it all came back to me, the memory of the long summers we had spent up here, as borderline feral as the animals. We had been up there with our mother, had minded the cattle, while father and the grandparents looked after the farm down in the valley. This was either before I started school or else during the long summer vacations. I can't remember how many summers I spent up here, in recollection they've all merged into one single endless summer. The sun's shining, it's hot, it rains for days, it snows, everything is swathed in fog. Storms are whipped up and we drive the cows into the byre and listen to them tramping nervously all night, hear the rain on the tin roof and the wind plucking at the walls of the hut.

It's a cool morning, everything is damp. When I get up, I can see Mother picking herbs outside. Half-hunched over, she walks through the meadows, her stick lying beside her in the grass. I step outside the hut and give her a wave, but she seems not to have noticed me, even though she sometimes seems to be facing my way. She's wearing a dress like all the farmer's wives here, with an apron and stout shoes.

The hut wasn't locked and I walked in and took a look around. I sat down at the table and ate the food I'd packed. I remembered the long evenings when Mother would tell us fairy tales and local legends by the murky light of a gas lamp. How the nuns acquired a lost soul from the Devil, and in return leased the Silberenalp to him. How he plowed the area with two fiery steeds, thus creating the karst, and then how the Devil sank into the ground in shame and dismay at his folly. I remember feeling proud that we were braver than the Devil and weren't afraid to spend an entire summer up here.

My brother and I loved being up on the mountain. We spent whole days outdoors, clambering up the rocks as nimble as wild goats, whistling to each other like marmots. We brought Mother silver thistles and strangely formed rocks, feathers and sometimes bones that we found in clefts in the rocks and that were all desiccated and white. We collected mushrooms and bilberries, wove wreathes from fern fronds and cotton grass and floated them on the pond behind the hut. We dropped stones in the well that was so deep we couldn't see down to the bottom. Only when it got dark did we go home to Mother.

It was during the last summer we all spent up on the alp that I decided to join the police. When they came to the hut, searching for my brother, I was only ten, but I never forgot their turning up at the hut, how they took over the premises, held their discussions, fanned out over the area, combed the karst in lines, how the dogs barked and their yelping echoed off the cliff faces, for hours, for days. But nothing that gets lost in the karst is ever found.

I still remember how we left the alp that final year. My father and grandfather had come up with horses to carry our things down to the valley. My grandfather led the way, then came the cows, then father, leading the horses with their load. At the very back were my mother and myself. Before we lost the alp from sight for good, my mother turned around one last time, looked back, and made a noise that sounded inhuman, a plangent wail that had something of a call, full of pain and without hope of reply. No sooner had the cry faded than I was unsure whether I had even heard it.

I sat in the hut all afternoon, waiting for the woman and children to appear, but no one came. Outside, some low clouds had appeared, rain was forecast for the next few days, perhaps it would be snow at this altitude. Finally, I decided to go back, so as not to be caught here overnight. The way across the karst would have been shorter, but the plateau was covered by clouds, visibility would be poor, and it would be hard to find the markers. I decided to take the longer but safer path that led around the karst instead.

The hut was situated in the middle of a wide hollow, ringed by rocks. I walked over the boggy pastureland, where the green was darker than on the drier slopes around, through fields of late-flowering cotton grass waving in the wind. The souls of the departed, people said, were caught up in the cotton grass, and truly they did strike me as a community of beings that had once dwelt here, and were whispering quietly in the wind, telling their stories of olden times, illnesses and storms, good and bad people.

The terrain grew steeper, then I found myself in a rocky area. The fog was wafting down the mountain, alternately wrapping me and leaving me and enwrapping me again. I could have been the girl I was, nothing had changed. I was a dirty, wild little creature, kicking out at rocks, singing to myself, plucking grass stalks and tossing them at my brother.

It had gotten much colder, and it was perfectly still. I could hear nothing but my footsteps, my breathing, the rustling of my windbreaker, and the occasional clacking of a stone that had gotten dislodged and was trundling away down into the depths. I felt alone in the way one can only feel in the mountains. When I stopped, I could still hear footfalls. I turned around, and maybe a hundred yards behind me stood the woman, who had also just stopped. She didn't seem to be much older than me, but she was wearing old-fashioned clothing and was carrying a stick. When I turned away and walked on, I could hear her steps, and I stopped again and saw that she was nearer to me. From now on, she stayed at a constant distance behind me, and even though I was out ahead, I had the feeling she was steering me through the ever-denser fog.

When we got to the pass, the woman without asking sat down in the passenger seat and let me drive her down into the valley. When I stopped, she got out with me, and we entered the station together. She asked where a toilet was, and somewhere where she could drink and wash. I led her to the holding cell, which is hardly ever used. I left the door open. When she lay down, I saw for the first time how inadequate the place was, far too small for a human being, far too bare, little more than a cage for a wild beast. A wooden pallet, a chair, a hole in place of a lavatory, a barred window, so high up that all you could see out of it was sky. The woman lay down on the pallet, curled up like a child. Later when I laid my hand on her shoulder, she got up without a word and followed me into the office, sitting down opposite me like my mirror image.

Where are the children? I asked. Time was pressing, the children had to be outside somewhere, the fog was thickening, and it would soon be completely dark. It wasn't a question of innocence or guilt, it was to save lives. You can't find anything out there that's lost. The woman looked at me, looked me in the eye for the first time. Where are they? Where are Luca and Annina? I have no children anymore, she said. They were seen, I said, we have had information from hunters and hikers that a woman and two children were sheltering in the hut and wandering around the region. I have seen children's clothes, rubber boots, stuffed animals, toothbrushes. I have seen their drawings. The woman smiled at me, full of love and sorrow. She did not speak.

I stepped outside the station and looked up in the direction of the pass, and saw the children, cowering behind a rock to shield themselves from the cold, how they defied the fog, the silence, the solitude. I think the way they do, I feel alive, aroused, living in the moment. I call out to them, they jump up from their hiding place, run toward me, throw their arms around my neck. They laugh and I laugh with pleasure and relief. When I stepped back into the warm station, I felt ashamed. I should have been outside, looking for the children, finding them.

We spent the longest time sitting facing each other, then the woman said, It's always the mothers who bring death upon their children. They have given them life, why should they not ask for it back? It's always the mother, she said. If there's not enough to eat, she sends

the father and the children out into the forest, sends
the children into the forest on their own. So that they
lose their way, so that the witch can cast her spell
on them, so that the wild beasts can eat them. I said,
There is no forest up there, and no dangerous animals
either.

Do you know the Chindlischtei, the woman asked
me, where the children used to come from? Whoever
wanted a child had to go around the rock and pray.
If you put your ear to the rock, you can still hear the
wailing of the unborn. I can show you if you like.

The woman was lying on the pallet again, she had
fallen asleep. I covered her with an old woolen blanket.
I imagined she was my child, I had to look after her,
keep her safe. I had never wanted children, I couldn't
have endured the worry for them. Every birth is a
death sentence. My former partner had failed to
understand that. There were other things he had failed
to understand as well.

The woman slept restlessly, talking in her sleep,
breathing unevenly. I brushed the hair out of her face.
I wanted to be there when she woke up. I sat down on
the floor of the cell; it was cold, but I didn't mind, I was
used to cold. The cell seemed to be less cramped now

that there were two of us in it. I leaned against the wall and closed my eyes.

I am in a cave, it's pitch black, but when I move, I feel the rough rock surrounding me, the damp, the clayey ground, the loose gravel. I can hear water all around me, dripping and splashing and flowing, sometimes very near, sometimes farther away. And then children—their whispering and laughing. I call out to them, but they seem not to hear me. I follow the direction of the voices, stumble, fall. I crawl on my hands and knees on the rough ground. The voices fade, then grow louder, sometimes they are right in my ear, sometimes distant. From the echoes I guess at the volume of the caves, some are as vast as cathedrals, some are tight, some are long and narrow fissures, sometimes it's not possible to go on. I have to lie down on my belly to get through the narrowest places, but I can't, try as I may, reach the children.

The morning was pitiless. The fog was so dense that you could only just make out the houses across the street. The road was wet, there was moisture on the windows. I made coffee and bought bread from the baker next door. When I came back, the woman had got up, stripped to her underwear, and was washing in the tiny kitchenette. I couldn't take my eyes off her. She had a fuller figure than I did, with heavy breasts and hairy armpits, her feet were dirty, as though she went around barefoot. She seemed introverted, almost meditative. As though she was performing a ritual.

I called the regional office, reported my observations of the hut, the traces of the presence of two children, Luca and Annina, and of the woman whom I'd taken in. My colleague promised to look for clarification and call back. When he did, it was after noon. They had tracked down the owner of the hut. He had explained that the items belonged to his children, who had left them up on the mountain for next year. He didn't know anything about the woman, my colleague said, but there seemed to be no reason to detain her. Are you feeling any better? he asked. I hung up.

The woman spent the day with me at the station. Most of the time she was sitting on one of the chairs in the entrance, but whenever someone came in, she retreated to the cell, as though not wanting to be seen. When I packed my things together at the end of the day, she asked me if she could sleep in the cell, she didn't know where else she could go. I couldn't refuse, but I couldn't leave her on her own either.

She washed in the same way as she had in the morning. I did too, and now she eyed me as I had her. But her looking wasn't covert, as mine had been, but open and full of pride. She smiled.

The pallet was too narrow for two. Come, she said and opened her arms. I lay down on top of her, feeling her warmth, her softness, her arms around my neck. I became quite small, seeming to burrow into her, her darkness. Her moaning, her panting breathing, her pain, her desire. A scream without hope and without reply.

The following day, my ex-partner came by the station. He was just wanting to check what was happening, he said, but I knew who had sent him. Whether I was doing better, he asked, if I wasn't too lonely up here. My only thought was to get rid of him as quickly as possible. In spite of that, I told him about the woman. I was overtired, he said, probably I just needed a rest. The station could stay shut for a day, there was talk of closing it down anyway. He insisted on driving me home.

He probably thought I'd ask him in for coffee. He switched off the engine and looked at me with a hangdog expression. I thanked him and said I was fine, he didn't need to worry about anything. No sooner was he gone than I walked back to the station. I couldn't leave the woman there on her own. She was still there,

sitting in her cell, smiling at me. I was afraid you would
disappear, she said.

That night was still deeper than the one before,
it belonged to us. The woman told me her name, and
now I recognized her. Tomorrow we'll go looking for
your brother, she said.

It was so foggy that I had to put on the wipers. At
Chruz the road was blocked off, there was a sign
warning of the risk of rockfalls. We left the car and
carried on on foot. At the pass, we came off the road
and struck out up the mountain. We passed the last of
the trees, ancient, gnarled things, after that there was
only grass and ferns and low bushes, then it was all
rock. We had to go into the karst even though it could
be treacherous in foggy conditions. We couldn't see
more than twenty feet but that doesn't matter if you're
looking for something you've lost.

In some places, the karst made broken-backed
ridges that fell away in deep crevasses and gorges, some
of them so deep that you couldn't see the bottom of
them. In other places all that was left was a line of
rock, which we had to shuffle along. Then sometimes
we had to overcome steep walls. I clambered on ahead,

gripping the rock and feeling in my arms the weight of the mountain and my own lightness.

I had long since lost all sense of time, the light was diffuse, coming from no particular direction, as though the sun had ground to a halt over the fog. It could be noon—or earlier or later. I can be a little girl, a young woman, an old woman, up here it doesn't make any odds.

Sometime I notice that the only steps I hear are mine, my breathing, the rustling of my windbreaker. I turn, but the woman has gone, I'm all alone again. It's my path, my fate, my brother I must find. It's my cry that is swallowed in the fog, my joy or lament, my ecstasy.

My Blood
for You

After the boss had seen a documentary about the founder of the Red Cross and had spoken of nothing else for a week, he sent the whole staff a round robin email telling everyone they had to give blood. About a dozen people came forward and went off one afternoon under his lead. I had pleaded that someone needed to stay behind and man the telephone. One after the other, they all came back, with a white bandage around an arm, so that the office looked like a field-dressing station. A year later, when the boss came into our little staff kitchen and hung up an empty list under the heading MY BLOOD FOR YOU, with the instruction to come forward, there were only four or five of us who put their names down. Just recently the list went up again. The new office intern hung it up and wrote her name down first. Bianca had the rudimentary and not quite finished beauty of some young girls, she was tall and very slender, with long black hair and pale, flawless skin. Her hazel eyes looked at you with a mixture of innocence and astonishment. Only the numerous piercings didn't quite seem to sit with her angelic being. When she introduced herself to us, a male colleague had called her Beautiful, and that became her nickname, among the men at any rate. Even though she was almost twenty and seemed to have experienced this and that. She had taken an introductory course at the art school, and there were rumors that she did coke—and earned the wherewithal for it by working for an escort agency.

I had lost a bet with an older colleague by claiming that Bianca's eyelashes were false. We women in general were slightly at a loss with the girl, simply because she was too beautiful. We made fun of the bewitched men who gave her all sorts of tasks, simply to have her near. Even so, none of them seemed to want to go and give blood with her, maybe because they were too afraid of fainting and making mugs of themselves. At the end of the weekly meeting the boss waved his list around and

appealed to our consciences. He, unfortunately, couldn't
make it this time, but that didn't mean that the rest
of us could bail. I said it was my period, and I couldn't.
I had no idea if that was true or not, it was at least
some sort of excuse. The other women looked at me
enviously, the men cast their eyes down on the table.
Finally, Herr Bruno, our bookkeeper, said he didn't
really have the time, he was bang in the middle of the
annual accounts, but the boss could put him down.
Herr Bruno was small and plump and thinning on top.
He must be past fifty, but he was still living with his
mother. Perhaps that was why he never touched alcohol
at any of the firm's functions, and in other respects too
he was sobriety itself. His family came from the north
of Italy, and that was about all we knew about him. He
was quiet and polite, and when there were arguments,
he stayed out of them.

Herr Bruno must have hoped his good example
would encourage the others to come forward, but in
the end no one else spoke up, only Bernadette, the
boss's personal assistant, mumbled some feeble excuse.
Looks like it's just you and me then, said Bianca.

It wasn't until years later that I heard from Bianca
about her expedition with Herr Bruno. She had

finished her traineeship and was still working for the company. At our Christmas lunch, conversation got onto the subject of the former bookkeeper, and when she and I stepped out for a cigarette, I asked her about what had happened. She was evasive at first, took a couple of pulls at her cigarette, and smiled mysteriously. But in the end she told me the whole story.

She had sat down next to Herr Bruno on the bus, which seemed to be unwelcome to him. At any rate, he slid away from her as far as he could, and when speaking to her, directed his words at the window. He asked her if she liked being with the agency, was she keeping up with her schoolwork, what her favorite subject was. He even asked me what my favorite food was, said Bianca laughing, as though I was a child. After Herr Bruno ran out of questions, they sat in silence side by side like father and daughter, and Bianca thought how odd she must look next to the little man, who was a head shorter than she was.

Neither of them had ever donated blood before and they didn't know what they were in for. The woman on reception gave them a form to fill in. They sat across from one another at a table, and Bianca peered at Herr Bruno's page to try and make out his date of birth, but she couldn't read his tiny script. Even though she weighed only a hundred pounds, she put herself

down for a hundred and five. She had to work out
when she had had her latest piercing, and if she had
taken any medicines in the past four weeks. I'm lactose
intolerant, she said, does that count as an allergy? Herr
Bruno shook his head and said lots of people were.
Milk wasn't designed for people, at any rate not cows'
milk. Bianca looked at him in startlement and turned
the page. When she read the next lot of questions, she
blushed. Did she have multiple sexual partners, was
she homosexual, a prostitute, or did she take drugs?
Herr Bruno had turned the page as well, and when
she looked over at him, she could see that he was
hesitating. Then he quickly made a couple of check
marks and folded up his paper.

They were then made to wait awhile before Bianca
was called. The doctor glanced at her form, asked a
couple more questions, and then sent her on her way.
While a nurse took her blood pressure and pricked
her finger, she saw Herr Bruno go on into the doctor's
room. Then she was made to lie down and roll her
sleeve up. As the nurse unpacked the needle, she
looked away.

She watched the plastic container which lay on
a sort of swing next to her slowly fill with her blood.
She didn't feel in the least afraid anymore, on the
contrary she felt light, only slightly chilly. By the end

of a quarter hour the bag was full, a whistle sounded, and the nurse came in, took out the needle, and put a bandage over the vein. You should rest a moment longer, she said, in case you get dizzy. Bianca looked around. The other couches were unoccupied. She got up and briefly had to grab hold of something, but the giddiness passed. She found Herr Bruno sitting at one of the tables in the little cafeteria, where the donors were able to recover and drink something. There were cardboard plates on the tables with chocolate hearts in different-colored wrappers. Bianca got herself a coffee and joined Herr Bruno. In front of him was an orderly row of at least ten empty wrappers. You were quick, Bianca said with a laugh. Herr Bruno said he didn't feel very good. He got up and propped his hands on the table. Bianca got up as well, and linked arms with him. While they walked arm in arm to the bus stop, Herr Bruno said he hadn't been able to donate. Why not? asked Bianca, then bit her lip. Herr Bruno said nothing.

He continued silent on the bus, only sometimes sighing or moaning. The idea that he might have had multiple female partners seemed absurd, and he surely wasn't homosexual. Maybe he frequented prostitutes? Or took drugs? She couldn't really picture it, but there had to be some reason, some mystery.

Herr Bruno said he wasn't going back to the office, he still didn't feel well. Bianca insisted on accompanying him home, and he made no objection. They changed buses and rode out to a suburb she'd never been to. Herr Bruno said he had some shopping to do, so they went into a small grocery store on the main road. Bianca carried the basket, and Herr Bruno put in a few ready-to-eat items: salami, candy, and a large panettone in a pale blue carton. At the checkout, he spent a long time burrowing through a cart full of half-price items that were nearing their sell-by date without finally buying any of them.

Herr Bruno lived in a block of 1950s flats. As they climbed the steps together, he said he had grown up in this very building. At the apartment door, Bianca asked him how he was feeling. You'll come in for a bit, won't you? he asked, in a wheedling voice. She didn't have the heart to refuse.

No sooner had he opened the door than she heard a voice go, Bruno? and a short fat woman shuffled out into the corridor. When she saw Bianca, she seemed surprised, but then she grew very animated and rapidly approached. She hugged her son and whispered—but so loudly that Bianca could hear very easily—You should tell me when you bring a young lady home with you. She had a heavy Italian accent. Suddenly,

Bianca felt a little anxious in the strange apartment with its smell of food and old people. She remembered American films where people who looked as harmless as Herr Bruno and his mother turned out to be sadistic serial killers.

The three of them sat in the kitchen, drinking tea and nibbling panettone. Herr Bruno's mother complained that it was much too dry and tasted of nothing. I don't know what it is, she said, chewing, but it's not panettone. She turned to Bianca and said her family came from Cremona, and did she know where that was. Bruno's father had come to Switzerland fifty years ago as a seasonal worker. Later he had come back to fetch her and their baby. He had died seventeen years ago now, of lung cancer. He worked with asbestos, she said, as she stroked the hair of her son. Now he was all she had. Herr Bruno's expression was hard to read, he seemed embarrassed but at the same time moved and full of affection for his mother.

It was more than an hour before Bianca could get away. The mother hugged her and kissed her on the cheeks and made her promise to visit them again soon. Herr Bruno walked very slowly down the stairs ahead of her. He seemed like an old man to her. At the foot of the stairs, he shook hands with Bianca. I don't know what my mother's imagining, he said, but I would be

glad if you would come see us again. Do you feel any
better? asked Bianca. Herr Bruno shook his head.

The next day, the mother called the office and
said her son was ill. He didn't come in all that week
and all the next week either. The secretaries passed
the hat around for flowers, and Bianca was detailed
to deliver them. Before she went, the boss called her
in to him and shut the door behind her. He said he
didn't know what the matter with Herr Bruno was, but
the bookkeeper was apparently going to be off for an
extended period of time. She should try and find out
what the matter was.

On her second visit, Bianca wasn't able to learn
much either. Herr Bruno's mother thanked her
for the flowers and said really it should be her son
giving her flowers. Then she cried a little, and said
he really wasn't well. No, Bianca couldn't see him,
he was asleep. What's the matter with him? His
mother sighed, put her hand to her bosom, and said:
His heart. Bianca asked if there was anything she
could do. Could I go shopping for you? The mother
hesitated briefly, then accepted the offer, and in a
trembling hand wrote out a shopping list that was
full of mistakes. When Bianca got back to the firm a

couple of hours later, the boss asked what had kept her so long. And you don't know what the matter with him is? She shook her head and shrugged.

Henceforth, Bianca looked in on Herr Bruno and his mother after work every other day. She shopped for them both, cleaned the kitchen, sometimes even cooked for them. She didn't even see the bookkeeper until her fourth or fifth visit. He barely spoke, whispered thanks when she brought him tea and cookies in bed. His room looked like a boy's. The shelves were full of thrillers and ancient hardback nonfiction books about foreign countries, aviation, and space travel. Herr Bruno seemed not to have any physical complaints, but he looked pallid and unkempt. Bianca offered to take him for a walk, and he agreed, even though it was already dark outside. Arm in arm they dawdled through the streets. Mostly, Herr Bruno was quiet, but sometimes he would point and say there had been a dairy here once, or this was where he had gone to elementary school. The author of the Sempacher song taught here, he said, indicating a plaque. Bianca said she didn't know it, and Herr Bruno sang in a cracked voice:

We sing a sacred song today
About heroic Winkelried

Bianca laughed, and Herr Bruno managed a mournful smile.

During subsequent visits, he became progressively more relaxed, and finally he began to speak. They strolled through the streets, and he told her how all his life he had been rejected. At school they had bullied him because he was an Italian, and so small and bad at sports. Even though he'd been good at school. He had wanted to be a steward for Swissair, but he had been too short. And there wasn't enough money for him to go to college. He was thankful he had managed to find a spot as an office worker. He had never had a girlfriend, nor really any proper friends. He couldn't even make the grade as a blood donor, he said, he was on medication for an enlarged prostate.

He seemed to want to get it all off his chest, and Bianca listened without saying much. When he stopped talking and stood still, she could see there were tears in his eyes. As if he'd been a child she put her arm around him and gave him a little hug. At that point she noticed something change within her.

I was still standing with Bianca under the awning of the restaurant. It was raining and it felt cold. In spite of that, we had each lit a second cigarette, and were smoking in silence. What became of him? I asked. He got a little better over time, she said. But he was already sixty. He took early retirement. That's right, I said, I remember now. We passed the hat around for a present. What did we end up getting? A city tour to Barcelona, said Bianca. She said she had gone on visiting Bruno for a while longer, but since she had a boyfriend, she didn't see so much of him. Two years ago, his mother died, and he moved into a smaller apartment. I think he's doing all right, she said. He's always popping off somewhere or other. Just a couple of weeks ago, I got a card from him, from Málaga. A few of us actually thought there was something going on between you two, I said, laughing. Bianca didn't say anything and smiled dreamily. Then she put out her cigarette and said: What if there was? If I've learned anything in my life, it's that in love it's not experience that counts but devotion.

Shipwreck

*Upon the whole, here was an undoubted
testimony that there was scarce any condition in
the world so miserable but there was something
negative or something positive to be thankful for
in it.*

Daniel Defoe

For dessert, Richard ordered the wild bilberries
with cucumber, ginger, and celery root. Lunch
was a dream, he said to the chef who had come out
to say hello. Richard hesitated. Though didn't we use
to dream of other things than lunch, once? The chef
smiled politely and wished Herr Gerster a pleasant day.

Richard's cellphone had gone off a couple of times
during the meal, but he waited till now to open it,
taking it over to the parapet of the terrace. For the
past few days it had been extremely hot, and the city
and the lake were covered in atmospheric haze, while
the mountains had completely disappeared. From the

lower terrace the sound of music reached him, and even though Richard had been expecting the margin call, he at first didn't understand what his stockbroker was telling him. Just tell me in words of one syllable, he said. Then he asked a couple of questions and hung up.

The room was littered with newspapers and printouts of newsletters, while the screen on his laptop had several windows open to various charts and graphs. Richard had instructed the maid not to touch anything, now he tidied up himself, dropped the papers in the bin, and logged out of the computer. Then he got undressed, slipped into the white hotel dressing gown, and went to the spa in the basement.

He would stay at the Dolder a couple of times a year when he visited Zurich to see his bankers. The meetings never lasted long; they were more like courtesy visits. Richard managed his money himself and conducted the transactions over the phone. There was just one time when Silvia had accompanied him, but she found it stultifying, and asked him why he didn't use a hotel in the center, that would be much more convenient. It's not as though you use the wellness facilities. It's the number one hotel in the city, Richard said, as though that was justification. The next time he went there, he was on his own again.

———

The pool was empty. Richard swam a few lengths and then stepped outside to the whirlpool. On one of the sun loungers that were ranked in the shade of parasols lay a tanned young woman in a gold bikini, leafing through a fashion magazine in a desultory way. Richard pulled one of the chairs out of the shade and lay down on it. He couldn't remember the last time he had lain in the sun. His skin was white, his body out of shape and clearly marked by indulgence. He felt the rays scorch his skin and sweat trickle down his forehead. After perhaps half an hour, a bald man came out and joined the woman in the gold bikini. They spoke Russian together. Richard jumped in the frigidarium to cool off.

When he looked in at the fitness studio, one of the women from the front desk came up to him. Is there something here that I can explain to you? she asked. Richard looked at all the intimidating equipment and shook his head. I just wanted to take a look—see what I've been missing all these years, he said. The employee said the hotel offered courses as well, fitness, Pilates, Antara, body pump. Richard said he'd never heard of any of them. Yoga, then? she suggested with a smile. He shook his head and thanked her. He spent the rest

of the afternoon examining the hotel's art collection.
He had walked past the paintings which were hung all
over the hotel, probably dozens of times, but only now
did he seem to take them in. He asked for a catalogue
from the front desk and studied one work after another.
The one he looked at longest was a couple of pieces of
cardboard that the artist must have cadged off some
panhandler and stuck in a gold frame. TRAVELING
BROKE AND HUNGRY ANYTHING HELPS
THANK U, it said on one. The freedom of beggars had
always unsettled him.

He thought he ought to give Silvia a call to tell her
what had happened. That he had taken out a Lombard
credit against his securities and lost all the money in
currency speculations. Eighty million down the pan
in a fortnight. Unless he got hold of ten million from
somewhere within the next twenty-four hours, the
bank would cash his holding and close his accounts.
The house would go under the hammer, and the
holiday house as well. And that was about as far as
Richard was prepared to think at the moment.

He settled himself in one of the chairs in the lobby.
The place was full of American retirees, presumably
part of some tour group. They drank beer and held
loud conversations about luxury watches, the low dollar
exchange rate, and the unbearable heat. Richard felt

like a con artist, an interloper who no longer had any
business being here. When the waiter stepped up and
asked him if he wanted anything, he shook his head
and got up. He went into the library and browsed
through the shelves, all travel literature, diaries from
expeditions, and magnificent illustrated volumes about
remote parts of the world. He was put in mind of a
landscape architect who had once said reading was
the last adventure you could have. In amongst the
gleaming bindings was an incongruous paperback,
Robinson Crusoe, by Daniel Defoe. Richard had read it
when he was a boy and loved it more than anything.
For a while he had thought about going to sea, but
finally he had gone to law school instead, and later
took over his father's business. He spent the rest of
the afternoon up in his suite, reading. He canceled his
dinner reservation for that night and ordered a club
sandwich and a bottle of wine on room service. He was
so gripped by the story that he laid the book next to
his plate and went on reading.

In the dead of night, Richard woke up and stepped out
onto the balcony. It was still warm, even though it was
long past midnight. The lights were flickering on the
opposite side, and along the shore the storm warning

system was blinking. He had never felt the beauty of the view as much as now. He felt he was like Robinson on a desert island from which there was no getting away.

He went back to bed and picked up the book off the bedside table. *It was in vain to sit still and wish for what was not to be had* was the place he had gotten to, marking it with his ballpoint pen, *and this extremity roused my application.*

As it got light, Richard was sitting at the desk, making a list of the kind Robinson had drawn up, of the advantages and disadvantages of his situation. "I have lost everything. I am ruined," he wrote in the column headed "Bad," and right next to it, in the column marked "Good," "But I'm alive."

He had spread out all his belongings on the bed, and along with them the contents of the minibar and the fruit bowl, the toiletry articles from the bathroom, the two courtesy umbrellas from the closet. Even the old newspapers he had fished out of the bin and laid out as well, you never knew what you might want them for. He made a list of all the things he owned and felt strangely heartened.

For the following days, Richard did not leave his room. Since his belongings were all over the bed, he made himself a new sleeping place on the sofa. He

carefully wrapped what was left over from his room
service meals in Kleenex and put it on the bed along
with his other things. He spent most of his time either
reading *Crusoe* or sitting on the balcony, staring into
the distance. He had switched off his cellphone after
it started ringing continuously. When the downstairs
reception tried to put a call through to his room, he
said he was too busy to speak to anyone.

That night a violent storm raged. The next day
the sky was full of clouds, and it was much cooler,
even after the sun came out. It seemed that summer
was finally over. Shortly after ten, the hotel manager
knocked on Richard's door and asked to speak to
him, but Richard didn't admit him, and didn't reply to
any of the questions and demands that came muffled
through the door. At twelve the manager reappeared
alongside the waiter who was bringing him his lunch.
Richard asked him sharply to leave. Once he was alone
again, he bolted the door. From now on he ordered no
more meals and lived off what he had accumulated.
When that was used up, he wrapped himself in his
dressing gown and sat down on the balcony, with
his eyes on the horizon, as though a ship might turn
up there to free him from his awful predicament.
Robinson lasted for all of twenty-eight years, thought
Richard, whose adventure had only just begun.

Peter Stamm is the author of the novels *The Sweet Indifference of the World, To the Back of Beyond, All Days Are Night, Seven Years, On a Day Like This, Unformed Landscape, Agnes,* and the short-story collections *We're Flying* and *In Strange Gardens and Other Stories.* His award-winning books have been translated into more than thirty languages. For his entire body of work and his accomplishments in fiction, he was short-listed for the Man Booker International Prize in 2013, and in 2014 he won the prestigious Friedrich Hölderlin Prize. He lives in Switzerland.

Michael Hofmann has translated the work of Gottfried Benn, Hans Fallada, Franz Kafka, Joseph Roth, and many others. In 2012 he was awarded the Thornton Wilder Prize for Translation by the American Academy of Arts and Letters. His *Selected Poems* was published in 2009, *Where Have You Been? Selected Essays* in 2014, and *One Lark, One Horse: Poems* in 2019. He lives in Florida and London.